WINNER TAKES ALL

WINNER TAKES ALL

WEREWITCH™ BOOK NINE

RENÉE JAGGÉR

LMBPN Publishing
PMB 196, 2540 South Maryland Pkwy
Las Vegas, NV 89109

First US Release, October 2020
eBook ISBN: 978-1-64971-276-9
Print ISBN: 978-1-64971-277-6

Bailey "Nova" Nordin stood on the grass under the shafts of sunlight that filtered down from the scattered clouds. It had rained last night and earlier that morning, raising the humidity, but the heat of summer was waning toward autumn, and the day wasn't too uncomfortable.

Still, after how much she'd been exerting herself, her brown hair was slick with sweat as she stared across the field and reflected on all that had led her to this point.

I wanted to get out of a mandatory arranged marriage and save a nice, good-looking wizard from being turned into some Seattle chicks' breeding stud. If you'd told me that I'd have ascended to godhood by the end of it, I would've laughed in your face and told you were crazy.

Now, I'm being asked to stop the fucking Norse apocalypse. No pressure, though. Shit, what's a goddess to do?

Forty feet away from her, staring her down, Roland raised his sword. The breeze caused his golden hair to fly away from his face in a mass of yellowish spikes and whipped his shirt about his slender frame. *"En garde,"* he said.

Bailey raised her own blade and charged at him.

Using the magic she wielded as both a werewitch and a goddess, the girl augmented her speed, moving twice as fast as a normal human being would have; the distance between them vanished in a flash. She was practically on top of him, her sword flashing and thrusting.

The weapon in her hands resembled a classic European longsword, made of bright shining metal that was not of the Earth. It lacked a crossguard, however, giving it an appearance that was both unusual and elegant. It sliced through the air and crashed toward the blond wizard.

Though not a deity, he was a caster of greater than average power and potential. And then Bailey had given him an infusion of arcane might that had raised his profile still higher. He was effectively a demigod now.

And using his considerable skills, he nimbly side-stepped her blazing charge, slashing the blade he held to deflect Bailey's strong overhead swing and pull her off balance, so she stumbled past his position.

Roland resumed his defensive stance as he turned to face her again. The weapon he held was an enchanted seventeenth-century side sword, a compromise between a rapier and an arming sword. It was able to cut and thrust with equal efficiency, and an elaborate shining handguard curled over his knuckles from the base of the blade.

Bailey taunted him as she readied herself for the next attack. "That was fancy. You've gotten faster lately. I figured I'd bowl your ass on to the ground in one move."

The wizard smirked. "Not yet. Nice try, though."

Their blades clashed again, and Roland slipped the point of his over Bailey's guard toward her face. She recognized instantly that he wasn't putting enough force behind the motion for it to reach her face. It was a bluff to make her flinch.

She did feel her muscles tighten and her head draw backward an inch or two, but she held her ground, ready for his next move, which was to swipe his sword down and aside toward her arm.

Bailey pivoted to the side. Roland's balance was good enough that he'd be able to respond quickly, but she was faster. She brought her leg up so her shin connected with his lower abdomen, then whipped her sword down toward his groin, pressing the blade lightly against his inner thigh as he froze in place.

"Dead," she informed him. "Carotid artery."

He squinted. "It's the *femoral* artery, dear. I think the carotid artery is in the, uh, chest or something. In any event, if I'm going to lose, it might as well be while you're caressing me between the legs. Though preferably not with a sword."

"Yeah, yeah," she shot back. "Keep up that attitude, and I'll do more than caress your groin with it."

He made an "O" with his mouth. "Kinky. You are, however, unwise to lower your defenses."

A storm of freezing sleet erupted over her head in a tight-enough column that it startled her and obscured her vision without much affecting Roland. She launched herself straight back, dodging the wizard's blade, and retaliated with a fireball that blasted through the freezing mess toward him.

He easily hopped aside from it, summoning an arcane shield in front of and around himself for good measure, then tried to catch her in a crossfire of two horizontal lightning bolts that intersected to form an "X" of blazing white light.

But Bailey was already airborne, slashing her sword downward, directing its course through her magic. It landed at the point where the two electrical bolts crossed and absorbed their energy before spinning laterally toward the wizard.

"Shit!" he exclaimed, doubling his shields and rolling aside.

Bailey floated earthward as her fiancé narrowly evaded the powerful attack. Her sword crashed into the trunk of a tree, getting stuck after passing halfway through it and then unleashing a torrent of sparks and smoke. The tree burst into flames.

While the girl dived for her blade, the wizard summoned atmospheric moisture to coalesce around his own weapon, then flung it at both Bailey and the burning tree in a tight wave, enough to cause concussive damage or even cut through matter like a knife. Bailey shielded herself, ignoring the foaming white spray that collided with the arcane barrier as she pulled her sword free of the trunk. The leftover water extinguished the blaze.

Then Roland was upon her, his side sword lashing nimbly. Though the werewitch's sword was heavier, she had more formal training in fencing than the wizard did, and as a lycanthrope, her paranormal strength more than made up for it, anyway.

Their blades smashed together, each now trying to

overcome the other through brute force. They pulled them apart, and each sent a feinting strike at their opponent's eyes, only to lock steel once more, straining and striving against the other's will with waves of psionic fear and despair attacks.

Neither yielded.

They separated again, looking into each other's faces as they heaved for breath and smoke rose from the scorched earth around them. Roland gently waved his left hand in a healing spell and a soft green light flowed over the ground, undoing the worst of the damage so that the grass would return soon.

"Yeah," Bailey panted, "I'd say that's enough for today. We're at the point of it being a 'damn good workout.' But if we go much past that point, it's legit exhaustion, and it takes too much damn time to recover from that. And we don't know how much time we have. Can't be caught when we're weak."

Roland sheathed his sword with an unnecessarily elaborate flourish, though he missed getting the point exactly in the scabbard and had to readjust at the last second. "Well, I tried," he mumbled, then, "Yes, let's take a shower and get some food. Can't save Asgard from destruction on an empty stomach, can we?"

"Probably not." She walked over, planted a kiss on his cheek, and led him toward her truck, their arms linked.

Things at the Bristling Elk, the combination country-western bar and diner that had sometimes been called the heart of Greenhearth, Oregon, were quiet. They were moderately busy, but things were normal. Bailey smiled. The warm feeling of peace and familiarity...she needed it right now.

Tomi, the main full-time evening waitress, greeted them with a wave. "Hi, Bailey. Hi, Roland. Go on ahead to your usual seat, and I'll be right over."

"Thanks." Bailey waved back, and she and her fiancé headed over to their standard place, nodding or saying hello to most of the other patrons en route.

Bailey ordered her usual steak sandwich and fries, along with regular coffee, whereas Roland went with chicken alfredo and decaf. The plan, they agreed, was to drink out of each other's cups half the time so each of them would get some caffeine, but not too much.

Tomi laughed. "Whatever. I'll bring you a third cup to mix it if you want. Anyway, I'm happy that things are finally getting back to normal around here. By the way, I haven't seen your brothers in a while?"

Bailey shrugged. "They must not be hungry. And business is good." Everyone knew that Tomi had a crush on all three of them, or at least on Jacob and Russell, the elder two.

The couple chatted about cars, sports, and the weather as they waited for their meals. Roland had first come to Greenhearth in the spring, and he was curious about what winters were like here in the mountains, compared to his hometown of Seattle.

"Ehh," Bailey told him, "they vary. Probably colder and snowier some days, and warmer and drier others. We're not far enough east to be completely out of the stereotypical PNW climate zone, so it isn't likely to be that different from Seattle."

"Hmm." He sipped his half-caff coffee. "I'd expected them to be comparable to Siberia, but perhaps not. Your summers are certainly hotter than ours are. Was hotter, anyway."

Tomi brought out their food, wished them a nice meal, and excused herself. They thanked her and dug in.

A minute or two later, someone wandered into the diner. Bailey's finely-honed senses picked up slight abnormalities in the person's tread and demeanor. She turned at the same time she noticed Roland, who was facing toward the diner's entrance, widening his eyes.

It was Loki. Today he was a slender, pale man in a dark coat with black hair, the mortal guise of the Norse god of mischief.

"Well," Bailey murmured, swallowing a mouthful of beef and bread, "this oughta be good."

Various other patrons turned to look at the odd man as he strode by. He had a way of attracting attention to himself despite moving smoothly and with minimal noise.

Loki stood beside their table. "Good evening," he stated in his low, smooth voice, pinching a steak fry off of Bailey's plate, sniffing it, and popping it into his mouth.

"Oh," Roland reacted, flapping his hand in annoyance, "just help yourself then, by all means. Take whatever you want."

The deity smirked. "If you insist." He picked up Bailey's fork, which she wasn't using, and stabbed it into Roland's pasta, twirling it around and adding a chunk of chicken to the tines before sampling it. "Not bad. Not superb, but acceptable."

The werewitch looked up at him. "So, why are you here? I'm hoping for good news, but not holding out *much* hope, we'll say."

"Oh, ha! Good news!" Loki chortled. "No, no, of course not. But not bad news either. I merely wanted to check in and see how you were doing."

Bailey shrugged. "Fine. Keeping up with our training and staying alert, but also trying to get enough rest, that kind of thing. Working at the auto shop sometimes. I'd rather make money the honest way than conjure it out of thin air. Shouldn't you be hiding somewhere, though? In case you-know-who appears out of nowhere? He doesn't know you've been sneaking around and helping us, and I'm pretty sure he'd have a few objections to that."

Turning his eyes to the ceiling, Loki pointed out, "Well, he has objections to *everything*, doesn't he? My existence, for example, among many, many other things. Anyhow, what exactly have you been training in? I'm curious."

Roland answered him. "Magic and swordsmanship, most recently. I'd say I have more of a knack for the latter than I would have guessed."

"Oh," Loki replied, "good, I suppose. Don't forget the subtler arts, though. This struggle won't be won solely by brute force. Subterfuge is a powerful factor." He arched his black eyebrows to emphasize the point.

The girl had to agree with that. After all, Fenris had employed layers upon layers of deception in order for his plans to advance as far as they had.

"Yeah, I know," she told the god. "We've been planning

and drilling ourselves in what to do and say if we have to play along, or if he asks us certain awkward questions. And how to slip quietly through an area without being seen. I only hope it's enough."

Loki flexed the long fingers of his left hand. "Perhaps it will be. You're better positioned for the task to come than anyone else. You have a good shot, though of course, nothing is certain. And on that note, I lied. Sorry! I did, in fact, come here to warn you and deliver bad news."

Roland threw up his hands and shook his head. "For fuck's sake."

Grimacing, Bailey responded, "All right then, let's hear it." She pretty much knew what he was going to say.

The traces of amusement left the trickster god's thin face.

"I suspect that Fenris is moving to trigger Ragnarök sooner than anticipated. Exactly how soon, I cannot say, but we believe he's taken to lurking within Asgard, our homeworld. Our agents have spied him here and there, under 'innocent' circumstances, but that is all. He's keeping a low profile, not making a scene. Slowly but surely, he is setting up the ritual that will culminate in his self-sacrifice."

Bailey gave a single slow nod at that. They all knew that Fenris' real plan was to sacrifice *her* in his place.

"And," Loki continued, "once that little shenanigan is completed, it will trigger the Norse apocalypse, leading to the end of Asgard and quite possibly its associated sub-domains, *and* perhaps your world, as well. Our dimensions are all connected, and the destruction may easily spill over from one to the other."

The werewitch rubbed her temples and closed her eyes. None of this was a shock to her at this point; she'd accepted it a couple of weeks ago. But that didn't mean she *liked* hearing about it.

Several nearby patrons could not help overhearing the conversation, and their hands began to shake as they gripped their forks and knives. The town of Greenhearth had suffered through witch invasions, wolf pack wars, and battles in the streets. The last thing the people needed to deal with was the end of the goddamn world.

Roland asked, "Okay, then why hasn't he made the final move yet? What else is he doing at the moment? There has to be more to his plot than only trying to trick Bailey into taking his place."

"Oh, ha." Loki snickered. "Of course. There is *much* more. While he was in your presence and you in his, Fenris seems to have forged alliances with the monstrous species that live in the outlands of our dimension. There has been an increase in border skirmishes between them and Asgard. We believe Fenris is behind this. It's likely the next phase of his scheme."

Bailey's jaw dropped. "Wait, what? You mean like the frost trolls and the dark elves?"

Loki helped himself to Roland's glass of ice water and took a sip. "Yes, of course."

"But," the girl protested, "I was with him. We went to their realms together to fight those assholes! How could he go from helping me kill a hundred of their warriors to making deals with their leaders in the same fuckin' excursion?"

Loki gazed at her with a fatuous expression that might have been a sardonic sort of pity.

"That's easy," he answered her. "He excused himself off to somewhere else at some point, didn't he? And the monstrous peoples are less concerned about individual lives lost, as long as they benefit collectively or their kings approve it. Fenris could have easily convinced them to sacrifice a paltry number of grunts in exchange for a share of the spoils of Asgard. All he had to do is *lie*, and he's been doing a lot of that lately."

Bailey felt her guts coiling up within her, turning to ice and fire in alternating cycles.

Fenris had been her mentor, her teacher, and her friend. Or so she'd thought. He had officially released her from the obligation to marry a random pack alpha by her twenty-fifth birthday, the Sword of Damocles that had hung over her head her entire life. He had freed her, lifted her up, and helped her gain respect in her community. They had fought side by side against mutual foes.

And it had been a lie.

She breathed in through flaring nostrils, calming herself. "Yes. I understand."

"Right," Loki affirmed. "Fenris will attempt to distract us with his hired thugs, and then he'll move on to something still more devious. For all our wisdom, we cannot say what, for certain. I don't claim to know what his final moves will be, so you must remain vigilant. But we, the gods, will be watching out for you, watching your back, whether in person or from a distance. You are not alone."

She sighed. "Thank you. You've done a lot."

The god of mischief grinned. "I have, haven't I? In any event, knowing that, enjoy the remainder of your meal."

He walked back toward the main doors from the diner. Bailey looked away for a second, and when she turned back, he was gone.

Roland stabbed his fork into the fettuccine on his plate, his mouth twisted with disgruntlement. "Such a *charming* fellow. You're right, though. He *has* done a lot to help us. I only pray it'll be enough. What about the others? Shouldn't we be hearing from the whole pantheon by this point?"

"Hell if I know," Bailey grumbled. "If I have to, I'll pop into the council chamber and ask them. After supper, at any rate."

Fortunately, that proved unnecessary.

The front doors opened and in walked multiple pairs of feet—at least a trio, by Bailey's count. She turned around to look and was impressed, if not exactly surprised, to see three more members of the divine council stride into the diner.

An old man at a table near the entrance stiffened and shook his head. "What in Sam Hill?" he blurted. The deities ignored him as they strolled past.

The three had not taken any particular measures to disguise themselves. Thor, the Norse god of battle, still wore a studded helmet atop his red-bearded face, along with leather boots and chainmail armor. Thoth, the Egyptian god of wisdom, wore a blue shenti and an ibis headdress. Coyote, the Amerindian trickster god, had assumed his mundane persona of a fiftyish Native man with salt-and-pepper hair and was dressed in blue jeans and a maroon shirt, but something about his eyes suggested the animal he represented in the pantheon.

Bailey called to them as they approached, "We were wondering when you guys would make an entrance. Wasn't expecting something this, uh *obvious*, though."

Roland waved a hand with a flippant motion. "Oh, it's okay. The good people of Greenhearth are used to supernatural beings barging in whenever they feel like it by now."

The three deities ignored the wizard's comment and congregated beside the table, as Loki had done, though they had the decency to refrain from picking at the couple's food.

On the other hand, they also sat down next to the pair, scrunching in against them. Bailey found herself smashed between the broad, dark shoulders of Thoth and the paler but even broader shoulders of Thor.

"Hi," Roland said to them. "Remind us some time to teach you guys about the mortal concept of 'personal space' and 'social distance boundaries' and things like that, okay?"

Thor guffawed, but Thoth only looked at the wizard and stated, "Very well." Coyote bit his lip as though trying not to explode into laughter.

Bailey pinched the bridge of her nose, though it was difficult to move her arms much. "Okay, yeah, fine. Loki was here five or ten minutes ago and gave us the general update about how he's reasonably certain that you-know-who will be making his move soon. Do you guys have anything for us beyond that?"

Thoth quickly reviewed the main facts, which, unsurprisingly, were about the same as what Loki had revealed. But he added something else.

"It is true," the lord of wisdom intoned, "that we shall support you, watch your back, and do all that we can. But for the time being, we must distance ourselves from the scene around you."

Roland, sweating from the heat of so many bodies packed together, muttered, "Great! Start distancing your-selves as soon as possible if you would, please."

The trio of divinities paid him no heed.

Coyote quipped, "We will sneak in when we're able to support you without being seen. Without revealing our aid and complicity in your quest to undermine the werewolf god. We must not disclose our hand too soon. Fenris must be allowed to think that no one suspects him and that he is getting away with it. Until the time is right."

"Aye," Thor echoed, pounding his fist on the table with what was for him a light, gentle pressure, though it was powerful enough to rattle the wood as well as the floor beneath their feet. "But we need a favor, Bailey. There's battle-work to be done, make no mistake. And you might notice that there are three of us instead of four. Balder, one of the few combatant gods, has gone missing. Vanished without a trace! Foul business may be afoot."

Thoth nodded and stared into the werewitch's eyes. "We fear Fenris may already have struck against him, and we want you to find him."

CHAPTER TWO

The large group of gods and Roland decamped from the diner and, once out of easy sight, flew to a secluded spot in the wooded hills surrounding the town. It was getting dark, and the trees covered them all with deep shade.

The deities collaborated on a psychic and magical scan of the surrounding area to ensure no one was watching. What they had to say could not be overheard by Fenris or his agents at any cost.

A moment later, they were satisfied that they were alone and no magic was being employed to scry on them.

"Okay," Bailey began, "tell us the rest. Like, where do you think Balder might be? Any idea? Any hints he might have dropped before he disappeared? I'll need *something* to work with here."

Thoth stroked his chin. "Nothing, in truth. No sign of him nor word from him, and we do not detect any traces of his specific magical signature anywhere obvious, either."

"Well," Roland interjected, "where does he usually go?

Or occasionally go, at least. Someplace you might expect to find him if he's not at your headquarters in Asgard."

Thor turned to the wizard and squinted at him. "We were getting to that, lad. If it answers your question, I was about to suggest the training grounds where we sent Bailey before she was permitted to assume her position in the pantheon. Balder manifests there from time to time, and especially when there's a bevy of new trainees, as there've been lately."

Thoth extrapolated further. "It occurred to us, and we discussed that the trainees would make excellent reserve soldiers if need be. Balder has overseen them before, and since most of them are demigods, half-breeds, or full deities who've not yet learned to use their powers, each is nearly as powerful as we are. One would be the equal of many dozen warriors of the monstrous species in a fight. We opted not to squander their potential."

The girl nodded. "Good, okay. Knowing he might be at the training grounds is a start. I've been there before and can portal to the place on my own. No one will be too shocked to see me, I think, but I'll keep a low profile at first in case you-know-who is around."

Coyote smiled. "You *have* learned a thing or two, haven't you? The old Bailey would have barged in guns blazing, wouldn't she have?"

"Hey," Roland objected, "we *snuck* into those warehouses when we were rescuing the kidnapped Were-girls. You guys weren't around for that, but I can confirm, as an independent witness, that it happened."

"Roland," Bailey added, turning to her lover, "no offense, but I want you to stay behind."

He blinked at her. "What? Why? Yes, you're more powerful than I am, but I'm getting kinda tired of you running off and leaving me to worry about you for a random stretch of time."

She ruffled his hair. "Yeah, I know, you'll miss me. And the feeling's mutual. But all I need to do is scout and see if Balder's around, and I can do that by myself. If there *is* any serious danger, there's no point in risking your ass alongside mine. We'd be better served by keeping you around here. People know, like, and trust you, and you have experience with rallying and marshaling them when that kind of shit is necessary. And we both know it might come to that."

He pouted in a way that she recognized as entirely sincere and heartfelt.

"Fine." He sighed. "I don't like the idea, but I'm smart enough to grasp the logic of it. Be careful, though. And come back soon."

They hugged and shared a quick, discreet kiss on the lips.

As they separated, the girl wished they didn't have to. She would rather have stayed in his arms and spent the night with him, and all the nights after that.

But duty called, and if the safety of their world could be purchased through her efforts, then at last, she and Roland would be together forever, inseparable. A pair, mated for life.

Soon.

She turned away and focused her mind on the gods' training grounds within the Other. She recalled the place's geography, its look and feel and smell, its vibe. She remembered the flow of its magical vibrations and visualized the place where she wanted to make her entrance.

Then she swept her hands to each side as though pulling open the doors of a cabinet.

An ovoid portal manifested before her. Its surface resembled slow-moving water, though it glowed dimly with the color of fine amethysts.

The girl gave one last glance at everyone present. She double-checked to ensure that her sword, handily cloaked from sight by magic, was still strapped to her back. Then she stepped into the gateway, icy cold and dizziness engulfing her as she was propelled through the astral plane toward her destination.

Two figures sat, quiet and unmoving, in a shallow depression in the ground. Around them was one of the most obscure, lonely, foreboding, and unpopulated places to be found in the alternate dimension known as the Other. The Other was made from the residue of spells and arcane entities. They'd settled here over the millennia, forming an entire sub-universe.

The region where the two men had come together was constructed specifically of the magical effluvium of beings who had died by violence.

The ground was parched and cracked, yet listless or petrified plants grew, as well as gnarled, impassive trees and thorny vines. Most everything was the color of dried blood or pale ash. They'd found an area that could accurately be described as a forest, dead though it was, with thick-trunked trees like columns of stone, their branches clotted with crimson moss or dangling dark red leaves like strips of bloody flesh.

Both figures were tall, though one was taller than the other, and broader of build. He wore a thick bulky coat with a hood pulled over his head. Only his nose and broad, square, stubbled jaw were visible, protruding from the shadows.

"Ragnarök," Fenris proclaimed. "Long prophesied and long dreaded. Sometimes dismissed, but no longer. We have passed the event horizon. It's happening, Carl. You would not be here otherwise."

The other man appeared younger. He was athletic, dark-skinned, and had an air of relaxed humor about him. He was a scion, the product of a union between a goddess and a shapechanger, and long ago, he had pledged himself as an apprentice to Fenris, god of wolves. He'd arrived mere minutes ago.

"As usual," Carl replied, "you're right. I am here, aren't I?" He laughed softly. "But you're right about the rest, too. That beautiful shining hall where the council meets will be ours. *The usurpers*; that's probably what they'd call us, but they'll be dead, so it won't matter what they say or think."

Fenris sensed that his protege was deliberately holding back on delivering the full report of how his last mission had gone. He didn't press him. He was savoring the moment, and with legs crossed and back straight, he relaxed, waiting for the scion to reveal the rest at his own pace.

Carl's fingers uncurled from his fist as he moved his hand to the side. Toward a slightly elevated mound of earth next to them, where a low table had been set up between two stumps serving as chairs. Atop the table was an old finely carven chessboard, with its two opposing armies lined up against one another.

"All the pieces," the scion pointed out, "are on the board. In place, ready to be moved."

Fenris smiled. "Yes. The contest will begin soon, and we have planned our game many, many moves ahead. We know how the enemy will react. Each and every step of the way, we will meet them, ready to neutralize their bungling attacks and remove their pawns. Checkmate will come soon. They will barely know what's hit them. Shall we begin?"

Both rose from their cross-legged positions on the hard dirt and sat instead on the stumps at each end of the small table. Carl positioned himself behind the white army, Fenris behind the black.

They began in a fairly customary way. Moving pawns near the middle of the board, tentatively, to block one another's movements and free up their more powerful pieces to enter the fray. Carl castled his king. Fenris did not bother, even after the space between his king and his rook lay open.

The wolf-god looked up from the board at his apprentice. "How is our friend Balder doing? Has anything...bad happened to him?"

Carl's fingers closed around the head of a knight, and he answered the question as he picked it up and moved it in an L-shape over one of Fenris' pawns to threaten his advancing bishop.

The scion commented, "He's lost. Hurting and on the run. I would not want to be in his position currently."

Fenris' hand hovered over the dark, glossy pieces on his side of the board as he contemplated whether to move his bishop to attack another piece or whether to assail Carl's knight with a pawn.

"That is interesting. I would be curious to know the details of the story." He repositioned his bishop to threaten both Carl's advancing knight and a nearby pawn.

Carl studied the board, making no move for now. "It seems that Balder was somehow shot with an arrow. By someone with sufficient skill and magical power to inflict serious injury on a god, of course."

The scion raised his eyes toward Fenris' half-shadowed face, and his smile mimicked that of his master.

"Ah," said the wolf-father, "I see. An interesting rumor. I will not bother to inquire further as to who could possibly have done such a thing."

Since they had both agreed that it would be best to take Balder out unexpectedly and from a distance, Carl had been practicing his stealth and stalking skills and his archery.

However, Fenris' smile receded somewhat as he contemplated what the scion had said a moment ago. Balder was on the run. He wasn't dead yet, but for Carl to have returned to report the incident, he must be confident of success. Fenris had forbidden him to return with a report of failure.

Balder was alone, therefore, and grievously and *mortally* wounded.

Carl seemed to sense his mentor's thoughts. "He will

die soon. It's only a matter of time until both the arrow and the magic take their toll on him." He moved his knight again, closer to the black side's king.

Fenris took the knight with his queen and handed the piece to his mentee. "Good," he stated.

"He's *finished*," Carl emphasized, seizing the knight and flinging it into the woods.

The lycanthropic deity responded with a slow nod of his head. "I am impressed. You have proven yourself worthy on many occasions, but in all honesty, I was not certain you could handle the job. It would seem that you have. Balder, still alive and free, would have posed a great threat to us. With him out of the picture, we're one big step closer to victory."

Carl chuckled and shook his head. His face was slack with borderline disbelief that it was finally happening, but his eyes twinkled with mirth. "Victory. Yes. After all the time we've spent preparing ourselves. What is the next *step*, Wolf-Father?"

"Next," Fenris elucidated, "we begin to gradually unleash the monsters of the universe, the exiled savage peoples and slumbering behemoths, against Asgard in a series of staggered attacks."

This was mostly review, and the scion bobbed his head in acknowledgment. His shoulders twitched with impatience.

"One at a time," the wolf-god went on, "in wave after wave, they will assail the borders of the divine realm, weakening the boundaries between their territory and that of the gods, and drawing the council's attention to them. That also means drawing attention away from us.

They will fear to look away from the burgeoning wars at their gates, and as such, they will not be looking at *me*. I will be beside them, inside their walls. It will be easy to get things ready for the masterstroke, the moment when they drool and sputter and struggle to grasp that *I have already won*."

Fenris took Carl's second knight with a rook, and in so doing, threatened his king. The game was not over, but it had suddenly grown more serious.

The scion frowned as he considered his next play. "I wish I could be there with you to see it. Perhaps I will be, depending on how all the details go."

"Perhaps," Fenris agreed. "Let us finish this game quickly, then make our final preparations. The End of Days—and, afterward, the Beginning—are upon us. Be ready."

The icy rush died, and Bailey stepped out of the astral channel of her portal and into a grassy field. Overhead, the sun shone. Thick, beautiful, old-growth forest like something from medieval England surrounded the sward, and a castle complex rose at its center.

She paused, looking and listening. Everything was quiet.

Under her breath, so softly that it would have taken another lycanthrope to hear, she murmured, "*Fuck me.*"

The walls and gates of the stone structure had broad scorch marks all over them as well as nicks, cracks, and gouges, as though blunt objects of great size and power had impacted them, along with fire. She couldn't tell how recent it had happened, but the markings hadn't been there the last time she'd seen the place.

And the silence was eerie in its flat, dead oppressiveness. No birds, insects, or animals sang or scuffled. There were no noises of sub-deities training, fighting, or feasting, as there should have been during the daytime since this corner of the arcane dimension had a day and night cycle much like Earth's.

Then she did hear something: the furtive tramping of feet. It sounded like two or three large, heavy entities and many smaller ones. The sounds weren't familiar, and she had no idea what might be making them.

She pulled her sword off her back, allowing it to wink back into sight, then took a deep breath and plunged through the opened gates into the outer yards of the castle.

Within, the sand and gravel of the lanes between buildings were trampled and irregular, and odd stains showed up here and there. Bailey sniffed the air, but her sensitive wolf's nose was confused by the profusion of odors. The blood of gods and demigods must smell different from the blood of mortals.

She rounded a corner toward the manor-hall where she had bunked during her training and found herself staring at the backs of almost two dozen monstrosities. They heard her and turned around, leering.

Bailey raised her sword as she took in the sight.

Three of the creatures stood around twelve feet tall. They were ungainly, misshapen beasts that roughly resembled men, though with the body proportions of apes, and they were covered with curly hair the color of dark copper. Their huge mouths were filled with rows upon rows of bent, jagged, and crooked teeth, and they hoisted weapons like stone-headed mattocks in their big, bony fists.

The others, numbering fifteen or twenty, stood closer to three or four feet, and were similarly ghoulish-looking, though they were squatter and their skin a vaguely reptilian green. They held spears with barbed heads or crude scimitars and set to squealing and hooting at the sight of prey.

Shit, she thought. *Ogres and goblins? I don't know if that's what they're officially called, but it's damn well close enough. Let's see if their bite matches their bark.*

The monsters charged.

Bailey stabbed her sword skyward, summoning a bolt of lightning surrounded by a cyclone of plasma, then used the blade to direct it toward her enemies. The blazing line of death struck the front lines of the advancing horde. Two of the ogres had gotten out in front due to their longer stride, along with six or seven of the goblins, and all exploded in flaming columns of light and smoke that scattered charred debris and dust to the sides.

The remainder of the beasts plowed ahead, jumping over the ruins of their brethren in their mindless bloodlust. Bailey drew her lips back from her teeth and plunged into them.

She surrounded herself with an adaptive shield that protected her from the monsters' blows or bowled them physically aside with arcane force. Meanwhile, she hacked, thrust, and sliced her way through them. The divine longsword did its grim work with smooth efficiency, splitting goblins apart two and three at a time.

A great ogre swung its mattock at her, and she jumped

and tumbled backward to avoid it. In midair, she conjured a lightning bolt that struck the beast full in the chest, causing it to go into spasms and drop its weapon while the remaining goblins piled ahead.

Bailey landed on her feet and quickly cut down the smaller creatures, then leaped onto the ogre's shoulders to spike her sword downwards through its skull. The blade absorbed the lingering electricity, and the giant toppled to the ground with a sighing grunt.

The girl hopped off the body and checked for any more attackers. She'd slain them all, and no others were in immediate sight, but she thought she heard more sounds of movement from the castle's inner courtyard.

Where did Fenris dig these bastards up, I wonder? A flicker of cold went down her spine at the prospect of all the minions he could have recruited. *Is it possible that they have nothing to do with him?*

It was, she supposed, *possible*...but she doubted it.

The girl launched herself into the air again, and this time, she flew over the wall of the inner bailey so she could observe the scene from above before descending to deal with it face-to-face.

Looking down, she saw a group of students, five of them, huddled into the corner between an outbuilding and the inner wall. Four of them appeared to be wounded and had trailed blood through the dirt as they'd tried to hide.

Another group of monsters, three more ogres and another twenty goblins, had caught sight of them and were charging toward their pitiful hiding place to finish them off.

"Hey!" the werewitch shouted, directing her voice

straight at them. Both the students and the creatures moving in for the kill looked up with wide, disbelieving eyes.

Bailey crashed into the midst of the monsters, her sword splitting the tallest ogre in half lengthwise and scattering the others with the small shockwave of her impact. She threw out a circular wave of fire that incinerated most of them while they were stunned.

The one student who wasn't wounded, a burly young man who might have been South Asian, rushed to join the werewitch, clobbering a pair of goblins near the front of the formation. Meanwhile, Bailey was a tornado of wrath, wheeling around with her sword, shielding herself with both arcane barrier-matter and electricity. She shifted instantly into her human-sized wolf form to pounce at the last goblin as it tried to flee. In a few more seconds, it was over.

The girl and the young man stood heaving, and the other four trainees gawked. Bailey stood up, becoming once again a woman in the same motion, and caught their eyes. Shapeshifting always did partial damage to her clothes, but she'd disciplined the ways in which her form altered enough that they still covered her body.

"Are you well enough to move? We need to get out of the open and into the keep." She gestured toward the tall secure stone structure at the center of the castle complex.

The quartet nodded, though one of them looked bad enough that she wasn't so sure. Remembering what Roland had taught her about healing magic, she cast a wave of soft greenish light on him to relieve his pain and speed up his recovery. Then she led the five across the courtyard and in through the battered and loose-hanging front doors of the central tower.

Once inside, the trainees collapsed against a tapestry hanging on the left wall of the entranceway. Bailey helped the uninjured man fetch a pail of water and cups for the others.

While they completed the simple task, the student remarked, "Thank you. I suppose in return for saving us, you want to know what happened."

"Yup," Bailey confirmed. "I do."

CHAPTER THREE

The council chamber of the gods was a high-vaulted room of blue and white crystal, with a translucent skylight looking out on a vast expanse of airy sapphire void and rolling ivory clouds. It was expansive, with a broad audience floor in front of the semicircle of massive chairs where the six deities of the council sat, and beyond the floor was a translucent barrier that provided privacy from the hallway beyond.

The hall had neither entrances nor exits unless one knew how to get there to begin with.

For the time being, two of the half-dozen chairs in the great chamber were empty. Bailey was not present to occupy the seat that had previously belonged to the Norse goddess Freya, and Balder was also unaccounted for. Thor, Loki, Thoth, and Coyote were all present. They settled in and prepared for the solemn discussion to come.

Thoth steepled his fingers and cleared his throat. The council had no leader whose authority superseded that of any other member, but as the oldest and most level-headed of them, the Egyptian lord of wisdom usually acted as spokesman, moderator, and master of ceremonies.

"Are we in agreement, then?" he inquired as Coyote watched him with bright eyes, "that Fenris is the likely culprit behind Balder's disappearance?"

Votes of "yea" went around the room.

Thoth nodded his sleek dark head. "It is the only explanation that is remotely likely, and yet, we have no definite proof. If we haul him before us and charge him with a crime he has succeeded in covering up, we will do nothing except alarm him into being more careful. Or moving faster to achieve his aims."

Coyote raised a hand and suggested, "He must mean to maintain 'plausible deniability,' as mortal politicians call it. Most of the bloodiest work is probably being done by his henchmen and intermediaries, while he keeps his hands clean for the most part."

"Aye," Thor grunted, his bushy red brows descending in an angle over his blazing eyes. One of his hands balled into a huge square fist. "The skulking bastard intends to come after us one by one, doesn't he? Picking us off in slow, measured succession, striking at the moment when we least expect it and are least able to fight back! Ah, the wretched cowardice and two-faced nature of it! If we *can* prove anything, I'll wring his neck myself. Gladly."

Loki held up a hand, barely restraining a contemptuous smirk at the boisterous attitude of his fellow Asgardian. "Patience, friend Thor. There may be time for that, but not immediately. We have to flush him out. What better way, I wonder, than to bait him?"

Thoth frowned. "Sending someone in our stead would

not be nearly as effective, and it could lead innocents to be endangered beyond any need."

The skinny mischief-god laughed. "No, no, Thoth, I'm not talking about using patsies or decoys. At least, not living ones. Illusions. Projected doppelgangers, carefully constructed to be as convincing as possible, and imbued with our same powers so as to further reinforce the deception."

Coyote laughed. "Fighting lies with lies, eh? Fenris ought to learn how it feels to be deceived, at this point, anyway. And it may well work."

Thor chuckled, suddenly appreciating the irony of the plan.

Loki raised his other hand as he continued to outline the details. "If done with skill and success, Fenris can pounce upon our doubles and appear to kill them; he'd be unable to reveal the illusion except with extremely powerful magic, or if one of us is stupid enough to cancel the projection before he leaves. Thor, take note."

The red-bearded giant stiffened and glared. "*What?*"

Before he could protest further, Loki went on. "And as each of us seems to fall before him, we will, at the last instant, trade places with the double, making the illusion utterly seamless. To do this, I will handle the main conjurations, but I'll need each of you to channel your powers into the task so I can replicate you more convincingly. Failure is, I think, not very probable. This sort of thing is second nature to me."

Thoth allowed himself a faint, morose smile as the other gods chuckled.

Coyote slapped his knee. "Ha, ha! True, Fenris thinks of

himself as a master schemer, and I must say I'm impressed with his layers of foul deception. But can he hold a candle to us?"

"Of course not," Loki snorted. "He is my son—technically—and he may have inherited some of my skill, but he is no true trickster deity. He's not on the same level as Coyote, *let alone* me."

Coyote raised a paw. "I object to that last bit. But I love the plan. Let the wolf-father reap as he has sown. His confidence will burgeon into overconfidence as he assumes he's whittling us down. Then we will be able to surprise him after he thinks he's won and press the advantage granted by surprise."

"Hmm," Thoth mused, folding his hands over one another. "Yes. And furthermore, the mere fact of Fenris trying to murder us—or our doubles—proves his guilt. Each of us may be witness to an attempt on our own lives. Nothing could be more convincing than that, in terms of justifying the worst of our suspicions."

Loki's eyes rolled upward and aside within his head; the expression usually meant he'd thought of something.

"Oh," he added, "one other thing. Bailey ought to be brought in on the plan and act as our double agent. She and Fenris have a history together. Well, what qualifies as a 'history' by the pathetically brief periods of time to which mortals are accustomed. It would not be difficult, I think, for her to convince the great lycanthropic one that she's still on *his* side."

Nods and mumbles of assent greeted his proposition.

Loki smiled more broadly. "It would help further if she was present during Fenris' little assassination attempts.

That may not always be possible, but imagine the impact. It will lull him into believing she's still his loyal apprentice. And then, right as the bastard is reeling in shock to discover us still alive, Bailey will slip the knife into his back."

Thoth frowned and eyed the trickster-god sharply. "You enjoy such things too much, Loki. Treachery is not our way, but in this case, we face a greater treachery that could destroy us and have no choice but to respond in kind. Let us begin construction of these illusory doubles soon and disperse for now. There is much to do."

"And," Coyote offered, "remember to have a psychic message ready to send out the instant Fenris or one of his cronies jumps out of the bushes and we pretend to fall. We must coordinate our efforts."

Everyone agreed, and the council dispersed. Though confident in their counterplot, a pall of doom hung over the chamber. They had no way of knowing for sure if they'd ever meet here again.

Agent Velasquez leaned back in his chair, hands folded behind his head, staring at the ceiling air conditioning unit through his dark glasses. The unit came on, its steady mechanical purr accompanied by a blast of refreshingly cool air.

"Ahh." He sighed, his face relaxing in a calm grin. "Much better. And I timed it perfectly. Seven minutes, thirty-eight seconds, though it'll probably change as soon as the weather starts to cool off more."

The Agency's Western Sector Headquarters was located in Reno, Nevada, a location chosen for its relatively equal distance from both Portland and Seattle on the one hand, and Los Angeles, San Diego, and Phoenix on the other, not to mention being effectively next door to northern California and not too far from the Wasatch Front in Utah. Days in late summer were cooler here than what the poor schmucks down in Vegas, let alone Arizona and south-eastern Cali, had to deal with, but the afternoons were still hitting a solid ninety degrees Fahrenheit.

Velasquez's junior partner Agent Park scoffed. "Man, you got too much time on your hands. I guess let me know if some bullshit errand *does* come up because I'm in the process of dying of boredom. This is worse than being deployed in New Zealand or Alaska or something. Like I hear the guys out of Fairbanks at least get to hunt elk once in a while."

Park was new-ish, having hopped directly over to the Agency from the military and hoping to get more action. He'd been disappointed about half the time, so far.

The senior agent chortled. "I'll keep that in mind, Park. Keep fighting the good fight. You're a great American."

"Fuck off," the other replied, though without much venom. He balled up a misprinted piece of paper and tossed it into a blue recycle bin.

Then he sat up straight, adjusting his glasses and staring at the wall-sized screen across from them, which had suddenly lit up from idle mode due to activity. "Hey. Look!"

Velasquez swiveled his chair around. His jaw dropped open. "Holy mother of fuck. What the hell sector of the

Other are we viewing here again? Uhh, 3-A, right, got it. Looks like we're back in the midst of a raging shitstorm, Park. Wanna pop open a bottle of champagne?"

"Maybe later," Park retorted.

The screen showed a rough layout of a certain transitional portion of the Other, the point at which the swampy landscape closest to the mortal world gave way to a region of barren canyonlands. The Agency had been keeping a close eye on it ever since their brief but hazardous war against an army of eldritch crones created by the late witch Caldoria McCluskey. According to the wizards who'd tagged along and helped, the destruction of the crones' main power source should have wiped them out, but there was always the possibility of stragglers sneaking back to Earth and trying to replicate themselves, preying upon mortal casters.

Now, the crude outline of the bleak landscape was swarming with masses of colored orbs, indicating supernatural beings on the move, but they didn't look familiar.

"Man," Park gasped, "what are those things? Do we have, like, a handy reference guide for what half-assed colored blobs of light represent on this thing? They don't look like the witch-clones from a couple weeks ago."

Velasquez seized the screen's control console. He was a man who liked to relax when he could, but when there was a serious job to do, things were different.

Punching buttons, the senior agent flipped through different screen views showing various portions of the Other, all of which had access points to the world of mortals.

It was the same. Every screen showed what might well

be an advancing army—clusters if not hordes, a veritable migration.

"Fuckdamn," Velasquez sputtered. "I've never seen anything like this. I don't know what it is, but we need to find out and fast."

He and Park leaped up from their seats, the younger Korean-American agent adding, "One hundred percent concurrence rate here, chief."

The pair strode from their office, Velasquez getting on his phone to report all he'd seen to his superiors, while Park handled the task of shouting the news to other agents and random support personnel as they hustled down the hall toward the armory.

"Okay," Velasquez barked into his mobile, "we cannot yet confirm what we're seeing, but if it's anything *remotely* hostile, it puts us about at Defcon 2, you got me? We need eyes on this crap immediately, and two seconds after immediately, we probably need every single available field agent with any experience recalled from whatever the fuck else they're doing."

The voice on the other end barked back with clarification requests and miscellaneous expletives, and they didn't end the call until Velasquez and Park were halfway down the elevator shaft to the basement rooms where the weapons, body armor, and hazmat stuff were kept.

The pair suited up, pulling on the glistening outfits that would protect them from some forms of physical attack, not to mention offer limited resistance against magic and elemental damage. Other agents came down the elevators after them, the reserve corps within the HQ building. Early responder types.

Velasquez gestured to them sharply. "You guys. We're going in directly. We need multiple advance scouts to figure out what the hell is coming at us on each and every one of those screens, and we need you all to survive so we can hear the wonderful news straight from your mouths, preferably. Video footage is nice, too. Retreat the instant things get dicey."

They understood. In another three minutes, everyone was ready for battle.

As they ascended back to the main floor, a generalized message came over the intercom. It began by more or less repeating what Velasquez had just reported, then it moved on to indicate that the brass hadn't wasted time deliberating on the senior agent's suggestions.

"We will be recalling all available field agents," the voice stated.

Velasquez chuckled, though without much humor. "Finally, they realize I know what I'm talking about."

"Every available hand is needed on deck. Anyone with experience. This includes a recall of semi-retired senior agents and a fast-tracking of those who are still in the late stages of recovery from injury. We repeat, something big is going on. This could be the one we won't walk away from if we fuck it up, gentlemen. Over and out."

When the elevator opened, Park turned to his senior partner and quipped, "Fast-tracking the injured into a resumption of duties, huh?"

Velasquez smiled. "You know what that means. Not firsthand, but you've heard me talk about it before. Townsend's coming back."

"Ahh," Park commented, his tone appreciative. "Just in

time for him to be reintroduced, I would guess, to the center of all fuckery in the known universe, or however you guys used to put it. Am I right?"

"You are," Velasquez declared. "The walking shitstorm of the century, Bailey N. Nordin."

Bailey refilled the redheaded girl's cup with water and waited for her to speak.

"We…we didn't…" The young woman coughed, then took another sip of water and swallowed it with what looked like a painful motion of her throat. "We didn't even know what was happening at first. It was all so sudden. They had effectively won the battle, or most of it, by the time we were aware that we were under attack."

The others confirmed the red-haired girl's words. Bailey glowered into the flames of the fireplace, where they'd started a blaze with pieces of destroyed furniture.

The South Asian guy had briefly filled her in on the gist of it. They'd been sleeping when a vast number of the ogre- and goblin-like creatures she'd fought outside had stormed the castle from multiple directions, killing almost everyone in minutes.

It was exactly as she'd feared—a ruthless cut to the heart, a headshot delivered from a rooftop to an unsuspecting victim.

After they'd refreshed the other four survivors with water and soothing words, they'd moved everyone to the central den, where there were couches and deep-pile rugs, as well as the fireplace. The more seriously wounded got the couches, and Bailey covered them with another shower of healing magic.

To her frustration, despite being a full goddess, she was insufficiently talented to bring them back to full health all at once. Her talents ran more toward destruction. She'd always been a fighter.

Once everyone was calmed down from the lingering terror of the siege, Bailey had begun to piece together the overall story of what had transpired.

"The grounds," one of the kids explained, "were normally guarded. Sentries here and there and watchmen at all hours, but only a cursory force to stop lone attackers or perhaps small groups. And to sound the alarm. Well, they *did* sound the alarm, but it wasn't enough."

A man, who looked somewhat older than the rest who had taken a nasty gash in his left leg, added, "There were so many of them. Hundreds upon hundreds. They swarmed right over the guards and the castle."

"And," added the South Asian guy, "it wasn't a disorganized mob, either. They're not so smart, but they can follow basic orders and understand simple tactics. Someone instructed them on how to assail this place. Hitting all the weak points, knowing which places to strike at first to get control of the complex and cut everyone off from everyone else. Like hitting the right domino and watching all the rest fall down in sequence. There was no way we could respond fast enough."

The redhead concluded with, "As if somebody inside had helped them ruin everything."

Bailey's hand trembled around the stone cup she held. "I see. Yeah, it was a planned attack. Make no mistake."

There was a long moment of silence as everyone stared into the crackling orange flames, their faces crisscrossed by flickering shadows.

The man with the gashed leg queried, "Do you have any idea who might have planned it?"

"Yes," Bailey responded at once. "But I can't tell you yet. There are...other people who are looking into a few things. That's all I can say for now. We have to be careful not to, uh, blow our cover or whatever. But we're gonna figure it out, and soon. And then someone's going to pay."

The uninjured guy muttered, "Doesn't surprise me. This was an act of war."

Bailey was starting to feel mildly nauseated, so she decided to change the course of the conversation. Particularly since, while she considered it justified to detour to help these people, she still had her primary mission here to fulfill.

"So," she began, "anyone seen Balder lately? The Norse god of innocence and beauty. Looks the part, though he wears armor and carries a sword half the time, so I'm not so sure about the 'innocent' part. Some of you might have met him."

"Yeah," replied a boy with long braided hair and violet eyes, who'd barely spoken 'til now. "He was here recently, uhh, maybe two days ago? We don't know where he is now, though. He was supposed to lead an advanced class on combat and forestry training, but he never came back.

The werewitch grimaced. "And did anyone else go out with him?"

"Seventeen or eighteen students. They haven't come back, either."

Trying not to panic with worry, Bailey asked for the exact coordinates of where the Norse god's training course was meant to take place. No one seemed to have paid attention to the specifics, but by asking three of the survivors, she was able to piece together a ballpark estimate.

"All right," she announced to the five, "I need to go look for them. Stay here for now; later on, we'll send someone to check on you. The place should be well-stocked with food and water, and you can all get some rest. I'll put a shield around it that they'd need another god to break through."

She said her goodbyes and left, then proved she was as good as her word. Raising her arms, the goddess of both Weres and witches summoned a multi-layered magical barrier of massive thickness and incredible power that encased the keep like a solid crystal dome. It would hold for four or five days, she was confident. That ought to be enough time.

Inhaling slowly, she turned toward the section of the forest where the one she sought had last been seen.

CHAPTER FOUR

H is boots tramped down the earth and the grass and the weeds and his hair flew out behind him, occasionally brushed by the grasping branches of the dense trees. Sunlight filtered through only in pale and narrow shafts; mostly, the forest was as dark as dusk.

Balder stopped, willing himself to breathe as softly and shallowly as he could. His right hand clutched at the magical arrow embedded in his right shoulder. Its barbs were gradually transmitting a poisonous plasma into the ether that served him as blood, but he dared not pull it out. If he did, the arrowhead would explode, discharging all its power at once, making things worse, if not killing him in an instant.

If he left it in, there might still be time.

He listened; the woods had gone quiet again, though he'd strongly suspected that his pursuers were still following. They must have stopped when he stopped, knowing they'd be easier to hear otherwise and planning to gain on him little by little each time he moved. They knew he was wounded, lost, and alone, and that his strength was flagging.

The god of beauty had taken a dozen and a half trainees into the forest to further their education in fighting in the woods. If the rumors about Fenris' planned uprising were true, they might well need it. He'd come to the training grounds without consulting the council. They had been busy at the time, and they'd spend far too long discussing things and deliberating.

So, Balder had simply taken action.

And now his trainees had scattered, he might well be dying, and he'd been chased deep into the woods, beyond the farthest reaches of the trainers' obstacle courses. It was possible he was approaching the bounds of another realm within the Other, a wilderness unknown to the gods.

He started running again, summoning his divine powers of perception to guide his path, but his inner vision was clouded. The arcane toxins of the arrow were interfering with the functions of his mind, and an obscure property of the enchanted forest was making things worse. Ironically, the disorienting quality was part of why it was a good place to train young god-beings and demigods in forest-based combat scenarios.

As his feet resumed running, he faintly heard all the other feet that were still chasing him.

Onward he fled, dizzy, pained, and tired, trying to bear back toward known territory but never breaking out of the labyrinth of trees into anything that looked familiar. His pace slowed. They'd catch him soon.

Balder gritted his teeth, turned, and put his hand on the hilt of his sword. There was no longer any point in fleeing.

He resolved to face them and make a stand—a *last* stand, perhaps.

The gaps between the trees came alive with dark, slender shapes, moving with a sinewy grace that was somehow unnerving; snakelike, in a way. They were humanoids, lightly armored in black, with pointed ears, skin of dark purple, and hair of pale silver-white. They stared at him hatefully with their glossy, oversized eyes.

He was totally surrounded. Any narrow avenue of escape would take him between two of his foes, and more probably lurked farther back in the shadows. There were as many in sight as the trainees he'd led earlier, and the sounds suggested another half-dozen or so.

Four held black bows raised, with arrows nocked and ready to fire. For some reason, they did not shoot.

Instead, six of their warriors advanced with drawn swords. The blades were long, though set in one-handed hilts, as well as narrow and slightly curved. The way they held them bespoke centuries of skill, for the swordsmen among the dark elves were legendary.

But Balder was a god of battle as well as beauty. He drew his rapier, and the long blade shone with blazing white fire.

Three of the elves gasped and squinted, unaccustomed to such brightness, and Balder seized the initiative. He pounced.

With a strangled cry, for his shoulder pained him, he drove the point of the blade into the nearest elf's throat, wicking it aside in the same motion toward the face of the second. The first dropped to his knees, clutching his bleeding neck, as Balder engaged two more at once with quick feinting strokes.

Rather than dogpile him for a quick kill since they'd risk losing at least one or two of their number, the swordsmen hovered around the wounded god's periphery, jabbing and lashing with their nimble weapons like men with poles tormenting a cornered bear.

Balder flung himself at two who'd stumbled too close together; his rapier knocked aside their scimitars and he crashed into them, bowling them over. One was dead with the rapier's point in his heart before the other could recover, but the remaining fighters attacked him from behind all at once.

A curved blade cut into the golden-maned god's side, and he grunted in pain, stumbling back, as more swordsmen joined the fray, grinning cruelly as they observed the flagging strength of their lone opponent.

Now he had two debilitating wounds and faced nine instead of six.

He raised his burning sword before his face. "Come then! Pay for the right to say you've killed me!"

They charged. Willing, it seemed, to purchase his destruction at any price.

Bailey had opted to hunt through the woods on four legs instead of two, her sword lashed to her back all the same with a magical cord. Her wolf body carried her over roots and between gnarled trunks faster than she could move in human form, and her senses were heightened. Tiny details of great significance leapt in front of her eyes, ears, and nose.

She'd passed beyond the edge of the known training grounds when she came to the site of what had to be an ambush. Bodies were sprawled throughout a circle of trees, all dead. Balder was not among them.

Arrows were embedded in wood or earth. What looked like sword strokes had split sections of bark asunder, and odd burn marks suggested that powerful magic had been used here.

But something was odd. The corpses numbered only ten. The boy in the keep had told her that Balder had taken almost twice that number on his training excursion. It was possible he'd been mistaken, but Bailey didn't think so.

She continued through the forest, sensing and recalling that magic was disrupted by the nature of the place. She'd have to be careful, especially since her nose picked up the trail again with ease, and further scars of magic and weapons confirmed what the aromas had already told her.

Dark shapes materialized out of the shadows. They moved at a steady but unhurried pace, focusing on something ahead of them and confident that they'd find it. Bailey made out five or six goblins, seemingly led along by a trio of thin humanoids who were about her height. Their black armor and long white hair identified them as dark elves. They had moved to strike beyond the borders of their wasteland homeworld.

Bailey snuck up behind them, then stood up and shifted back into human form. She cleared her throat loudly, following it with "Excuse me!"

The hunting party spun to face her, brandishing their

weapons. "Who are you?" one of the elves hissed. "Are you..."

"Probably," she replied. "What's going on? You hunting squirrels?"

One of the goblins squealed, "Shut your mouth! Go away, you! Die!"

Ignoring it, the apparent leader of the elves sneered. "None of your concern, girl. You look familiar, yet we are here merely to secure our borders, which have expanded into unclaimed territory. We will forget we saw you if you turn back now."

Bailey glanced past them and saw traces of the trail she'd been following.

She put her fists on her hips. "I'm afraid I can't do that because my own squirrel-hunting activities are taking me in that direction." She gestured. "We could always split the squirrel between us."

One of the elves fired an arrow at her faster than she would have thought possible, but she'd expected as much and flung herself aside while covering her front with a shield. The arrow glanced off it at the point it would have entered her face.

The other creatures attacked.

Bailey unslung her sword and drew it in a flash, cutting the first goblin in half. Then she conjured a torrent of water that pushed back two goblins and two elves, freezing it solid so they were trapped in a cocoon of icy spikes that pierced their bodies in multiple places.

The last elf, the archer, shot at her again, and she caught the arrow telekinetically, turned it around, and launched it into the chest of another goblin. By then, she was airborne, her sword hacking down at the bowman's head.

One goblin remained alive, alone amidst the bodies of his fallen comrades. Bailey didn't move against him; she simply held her sword out from her stomach, ready to swing in any direction, and stared into the small creature's eyes.

Trembling, he first dropped his jagged sword and then fell to his knees. "Lady! Great lady, please. No kill! I tell you what want to know. Please!"

"Okay," she said, advancing two slow steps and lowering the sword. She kept it ready to bring up again at an instant's notice but figured it would behoove her not to actively threaten the goblin. He was terrified of her.

She blew a breath out through her nose and spoke. "You heard what I asked the elves. Tell me everything you know, especially about Balder. And about what your plans are, and who sent you here, and why."

The goblin's ability to speak in ways comprehensible to human-like beings was limited, and the fact that he was hysterical didn't help. By asking him to clarify things and parsing her way through the gibberish and broken diction, she pieced together most of what she needed.

Balder was indeed here, first and foremost. Under the leadership of an elite band of dark elf warriors, they'd been sent here to track him down and finish him off. The goblin didn't know who had given the order at the very top, and he didn't seem to care, either. As his fear subsided, it was replaced by an increasing wave of vicious excitement.

"Ragnarök!" the beast exclaimed, his green-lipped

mouth breaking into a grin. "Is coming—is here! Promised to us! It will come!"

Bailey raised her sword an inch. "Promised by *who?* And *when* is it coming?"

"Soon! Now! Very soon!" the goblin shrieked, ignoring the first question. "Asgard fall down! Gods all die! They dead, over, gone. Age of monsters is coming. Is here! We slaughter all! *You die!*" He bobbed up and down on his feet, too caught up in his sudden surge of enthusiasm to consider his position.

Bailey had heard enough.

She whacked the goblin on the head with the flat of her blade, drawing a sharp cry of pain from the creature, then kicked him into the nearest tree. He slumped, unconscious, probably injured. She couldn't bring herself to execute him outright while he was unarmed and had surrendered, but if he died later, she couldn't honestly say she cared much.

Jogging on into the forest, Bailey picked up the trail easily enough. Both the elves and the goblins were agile and stealthy in their ways, but the dark elf homeworld was mostly a rocky desert, as she recalled, and the goblins were too numerous and undisciplined. Neither was able to move through the dense forest without leaving some sign of their passage.

Not to mention, nothing could hide its smell from the nose of a wolf.

Soon the girl sensed she was getting closer to her quarry. Up ahead were the noises of sporadic combat, almost like a duel or a training session, which puzzled her. It didn't sound like an all-out battle.

The foliage parted before her, and she saw an area

where the trees were not quite as dense, as well as a dozen lithe, dark shapes in a slowly-moving circle around a familiar figure, who grunted, gasped, and struggled against them.

Her eyes bulged, and while gripping her sword in her right hand, she threw out her left.

Undulating homing bolts of plasma, bright reddish-pink, snaked out from her spread fingers, cutting through tree branches and masses of leaves and vines, finding their mark in the backs of five of the elves closest to her. The humanoids screamed or groaned as the projectiles seared through their spines and hearts, toppling them all at once.

Half of those who remained turned toward the new arrival, raising their swords, while Balder strove against the few who were engaging him with renewed vigor.

Bailey lunged at the first elf to challenge her. "Bastards! You're toying with him, aren't you?"

The curved blade of her adversary was fast, but not fast enough. She knocked it aside with a lightning-quick thrust and skewered him through the upper chest, then kicked him aside to engage the others.

Everything became a raging melee of violence, and both elves and tree branches seemed to fall at random. The world spun, then Bailey and Balder stood alone in the small glade.

"Oh," Balder gasped, "Bailey. I didn't think there was any chance that—"

She'd been grinning at seeing him still alive, but before they could celebrate, they were interrupted. The woods ahead of them abruptly bristled with black-armored shapes, shorter greenish forms beside their hips and waists, and curved swords for all.

"Shit on a shingle," the werewitch cursed. "I'm not hurt, so I'll go out in front."

Balder struggled to raise his rapier in a fighting stance; he switched the blade to his left hand so his shoulder would not pain him any more than needed. "Be careful. Beware of their arrows!"

One of the elves let out a dry, rasping chuckle. "We would rather not shoot you, though we will if we must. We have the opportunity to collect the heads of two gods instead of one, and the sword laughs with greater delight when it can shear through the neck of an opponent who still fights and strives. Beheading a foe felled with an arrow is not the same."

Bailey snorted. "If you want to handicap yourselves, fine with me." She raised her sword and *detonated* the stretch of forest where the white-haired humanoids had gathered.

The explosion projected its heat, light, sonic percussion, and kinetic force straight upward at the goddess' command. It did not resemble an expanding dome or sphere, but a tight rising column of fire and fury. The dark shapes of trees, elves, and goblins who'd been reduced to unrecognizable cinders showed through the yellow and white mass, then it faded.

When the smoke cleared, two elves and four goblins remained. They stared, open-mouthed, at the black circle where their comrades had been.

"Okay," Bailey stated, "that evens up the odds, I'd say. I hereby promise to fight fair from here on."

The six monsters howled in rage and lunged toward her.

She met them head-on, her longsword clashing with scimitars and knocking aside spears, its magically-augmented blade cleaving flesh and armor. Both elves and two goblins fell.

The last two of the smaller creatures rushed past the girl to attack Balder, whose rapier impaled the skull of the first, then he kicked the other into a tree before stabbing it through the heart.

"All right," he panted, "we've won for the time being. Please, help me to rest against a tree. I need a respite."

Bailey rushed to the god's side and took his good left arm, finding a trunk shaped in a way that he could lean his lower back and hips on it without irritating his wounded shoulder.

The girl examined the arrow. "I should pull that out. You can't heal properly if the damn thing's still in there, right?"

"*No,*" Balder urged, holding up a hand. "You must not. It's a trap, a trick arrow. If removed, the head will explode and suffuse the whole area with magic. Not only energy attacks but a variety of curse that can insinuate its way through barriers. It could do us both serious harm. I am already weakened; I might die at once or be left so depleted by the blast that a single warrior of the dark *alfar* could finish me off. It is too dangerous for you as well as me."

Frowning with concern, Bailey retracted her hands. "Okay, but we need to get you some help and fast. Do you think you can make it through the woods out of here? If not, I might be able to, well, levitate you and float you back, something like that. Or try to open a portal, though it seems like magic is wonky in these woods. Most of mine worked well enough, but it felt strange, like it didn't *want* to work."

Balder nodded. "Yes, they use this forest to train the recruits in fighting without magic. And the arrow has properties that have...interfered with my arcane sensibilities. I cannot see except with my eyes or summon any great spells."

The girl waited for the deity to recover a bit, then asked, "Who did this to you? Dark elves and their pet goblins, obviously, but who ordered it?"

"I'm not sure." Balder's lungs heaved, and he stood up straight again with difficulty. "I have no idea how they could have gotten so close without alerting me to their presence. This jungle is an easy place to sneak up on some beings, but I am rarely ambushed. Whoever did this knew what they were doing and was aware of how to get through my defenses."

A cold tingle of dread crept down the werewitch's spine. What Balder had said reminded her far too much of what she'd heard from the trainees at the castle earlier. It confirmed the suspicion, bordering on certainty, that the attack was an inside job.

Balder went on. "The arrow came out of the trees; I never saw who fired it. And then they attacked, the *alfar* and their allies. Worse yet, nearly half of my students joined them. The effects of the poison on my mind acted swiftly, and I could not respond fast enough. It was all so shocking. Ambush and betrayal at once!"

The girl realized that Balder was succumbing to

despair. "It's not over yet," she reassured him. "You're going to get through this, and so are we. And Asgard and Earth. Fenris' lies have spread farther than we thought. He must have corrupted some of your trainees. But this is all gonna end, and soon."

The blond deity nodded. "Yes, I suppose it must. We need to leave this place and decide on our next moves. You should find Carl, my apprentice. He was your friend during training; you remember him."

"I do," she affirmed. "I'll look for him as soon as I get you taken care of."

She paused, then, struggling with the logistics of how and when to get Balder to safety and how to arrange it so that she could see him cared for while also seeking out Carl as soon as possible.

While she deliberated, a portal opened in front of her.

Balder tensed beside her, and the girl reflexively fell into a fighting stance.

"Oh, hell," she breathed.

CHAPTER FIVE

Out of the shimmering purple doorway stepped Loki. A slight breeze caught his black hair and blew it aside from his face as he gazed down his nose toward them with his usual mixture of condescension and detached amusement.

"Ah," he remarked, "there you are. I'm glad I was able to pinpoint your exact location in this awful place. It interferes with magic, though more from within than without."

Bailey let out a sigh of relief. "Hi. And yeah, thanks, you're just in time. Balder and his students got ambushed, and I had to fight off a bunch of dark elves and goblins or whatever they are—green guys three or four feet tall. Balder's got an accursed arrow in his shoulder. Literally accursed, I mean."

Loki's eyes went wide, and the sarcastic-asshole demeanor vanished instantly. He rushed past the werewitch toward his wounded relative.

The god of innocence let out a soft, hollow laugh. "Loki.

Who would have expected that you'd be the one to come so readily to my aid?"

"Silence," the lord of mischief snapped. "Is that one of those arrows that explodes if you try to pull it out?"

"Yeah," Bailey told him. "Glad he warned me before I tried."

Loki pursed his lips, examining the projectile. "Mmm, yes, I can remove it. The ways of nastiness and deceit and dirty tricks, and all manner of similar things, are well known to me. Booby traps like this are elementary."

Bailey recalled how much he'd helped during their war against Callie's army of ghost crones, so she didn't doubt his abilities. Still, what Balder had said about the lethal burst of the arrow concerned her enough that she backed off a few paces. Just to be safe.

As Balder leaned his front against the nearest tree, Loki came up behind him and wrapped his hand around the arrow, not yet trying to draw it out but hovering his other hand over the wound and examining it. The werewitch assumed he must have been "feeling out" the arcane structure of the spell, unraveling the process by which it had been imbued with such powerful malice.

There was a faint yellowish-green glow around the trickster god's arms as he began, slowly and carefully, to pull the dart free. Balder moaned, grunted, and trembled in pain.

Bailey wanted to shout at Loki to be careful, but she knew better. There was no way to remove a barbed arrow without hurting the person. They were lucky that gods healed mundane wounds more readily than humans did.

Finally the arrowhead emerged from the wound along

with the shaft, and Loki tossed it gently aside, immediately encasing it in a thick shield-capsule that crackled with extra layers of arcane security. "Beastly thing," the black-haired deity muttered. "I have standards, believe it or not, and those arrows are beneath them. They are weapons powered by absolute ageless hatred."

Balder's shoulder was bleeding, and he seemed on the verge of losing consciousness.

"Stand up," Loki told him, pressing his hand over the gash to staunch the flow of ichor-blood. "I'll pass on a portion of my strength to you, as well. It will bring you up to acceptable functionality, but it will weaken me."

The girl offered no objection. Loki had empowered her in a similar fashion not long past.

"Bailey," Loki said, "the two of us will need some time to recover after this. We'll have to lie low, out of sight, and out of reach to offer you immediate aid. Do you understand?"

She crossed her arms over her chest. "Yes. Makes my life harder, but I can deal with that if neither of you will die."

Loki smiled. "That's the spirit. Let us discuss, meanwhile, the devious plot that we've come up with for opposing our mutual friend, the deity of lycanthropy. Meaning my bastard son, not *you*, Ms. Nordin."

"I know who you meant," she grumbled.

As Balder recovered his strength and senses, Loki sat down on a big curling root. The werewitch noticed that he looked pale and tired after donating magical energy to his brother.

"Now," the trickster god began, "listen closely..."

The girl did. Loki explained the outline of the council's plan to fake their own deaths at Fenris' hands and how he was confident in their ability to generate illusions that were perfectly convincing replicas of the original gods.

He went on to describe how Bailey might have to take part in the activities to come by continuing to play along and maintain Fenris' trust.

"Follow his orders," Loki instructed her. "Heed his suggestions. As I understand it, you've always been the type to ask a reasonable question or two about the *why* of things, so you don't want to appear *too* eager to do precisely what he wants. But keep doing as you've been doing. He must believe you're on his side and that you'd side with him instead of us if push comes to the proverbial shove."

She bowed her head, then raised it. "I understand, and I have to concede it's a smart plan. If he strikes, we know he's guilty one hundred percent, yet we won't lose any of you guys. And if he doesn't by some chance, no harm, no foul."

It occurred to her that though her rational mind highly doubted that Fenris was entirely innocent, part of her wanted him to be. She would rather keep him as her friend, her teacher. She hated the thought that they had to be enemies. She wished his lies were true.

No, Bailey, she told herself. *That's not how it works. We focus on doing what has to be done and protecting everyone else first and foremost. You can deal with your own mishmash of emotions later.*

Loki went on. "Given Balder's condition and the fact that whichever servant of Fenris' fired the arrow knows he's in bad shape, I'd say we should begin with a nice fake Balder and allow Fenris to chase it down and murder it. Tempt him into making a clear, present, and obvious attack in the open where we can all see it. That will remove the last traces of doubt from *all* our minds, won't it?"

The werewitch frowned deeply. "Yes. I'd imagine so."

"And," Loki added, "it will bolster the wolf-god's confidence and deceive him into thinking he's gaining the upper hand, exactly as he's deceived us time and time again. At least when I lie, it's usually for the sake of a joke."

Bailey waved her hand sharply. "You said that for the illusions to work properly, the real god has to be there first, and he swaps places with the double at the last second. Is that right? Won't that put Balder at massive risk if he doesn't time it perfectly?"

"More likely," the lord of mischief retorted, "it will be a *minor* risk. I think."

Balder turned toward her, his beautiful face strained with diminishing anguish. "There is danger, yes, but Loki is right. It is necessary and the best opportunity we've received thus far. I am willing to chance it."

The girl closed her eyes, again forcing her feelings aside in the name of duty. "Fine, so be it. There are more lives at stake than only his, after all."

Balder smiled. "Exactly."

Loki looked skyward and tapped his fingers on the back of his hand. "Hmm. And now a stratagem is forming as to how, specifically, we can lure our beloved Fenris into the necessary confrontation. Knowing him as I do, it ought to work."

"Let's hear it," Bailey urged.

Loki laughed nastily, his eyes focused on something far distant before he looked back at his fellow gods.

"What we shall do is deposit Balder somewhere on the fringe of a domain where Fenris is the ruling power, or at least the absentee landlord. That way, via the channels of arcane influence that experienced divine beings can sense, he will perceive Balder's presence, and more importantly, his weakness and pain."

Balder squinted. "But why would I go to a realm of his if I were wounded? His territories are nowhere near this one, and there are other places I could go if I was looking for help with my injuries."

Loki scoffed. "Who said you were looking for help? No, the kind of thing you'd do is march straight out there for the express purpose of *challenging* him. Summon him to you with a barrage of threats, saying you know what he's up to. The only way for him to silence you will be by slaying you. He'd enjoy it, besides."

Although the god of mischief sounded sure of himself, Bailey didn't understand.

"But haven't Fenris and Balder known each other for a long time? Does he actually hate everyone that much?"

"No," Loki replied. "Fenris doesn't *like* us much, but he is what you might call an 'apex predator.' By nature, he is a hunter. He's cultivated enough savvy and self-discipline to pull off this little scam of his so far, but his true urge is to move in for the kill. His motives are always directed toward that. In this case, to relish the challenge of pouncing upon, fighting with, and brutally slaying our poor, innocent god of innocence. The temptation will be far too much for him to resist."

Balder's face had acquired a grim smile that was totally unlike him. The werewitch pondered if the nature of the events they'd become embroiled in was teaching him the alien emotion of cynicism.

"Aye," Balder agreed. "It is a wise plan, and if done right, it will allow me to gauge Fenris' strength in the process."

Bailey shrugged. "Good point. But be cautious. Anyway, what about me? Should I do anything in particular?"

Loki chortled. "We shall see, as far as Balder's case goes. As for the bigger picture, you should *certainly* do something. Since I am the *smart* god, allow me to lay out what is likely to happen as far as your role is concerned."

Looking extremely pleased with himself, the prankster deity elaborated upon his predictions.

"Fenris will leverage all of the connections he's made against us, using their borrowed strength to try to keep us off-balance and preoccupied. It's tremendously likely that he will bring you into it to keep doing the good work of putting down rebellions by the monsters he's stirred up. This will keep you busy and also make it look as though he's still one of the so-called good guys, a heroic deity doing his part to protect the realms."

Bailey scowled. That was what Fenris had *been* doing unless they were mistaken, so it hardly qualified as much of a prediction on Loki's part. But there was more.

"Furthermore," Loki continued, "these shenanigans will clearly be used to empower you further. To increase your skill and experience and give you opportunities to absorb power from defeated adversaries. He must know that you learned to drain magic from non-deities not long ago and is scheming to turn that to his advantage.

"Don't be stupid though, Bailey. And by stupid, I mean 'humble' or something along those lines. *Take all the power you can get.* It will come in handy. Fenris means to sacrifice you, yes, as we've all surmised, and bringing you up to a certain level of divine might is a prerequisite for him being able to effect that. But it also means that as long as your guard is up and your mind sharp, you will be strong enough to take him on yourself. *He'll* be caught off-guard and defeated by the person he least expects to challenge him."

Bailey pondered it. It made sense. Part of her didn't like the devious, Machiavellian aspect of it, but Fenris, by starting a war of lies, had effectively forced them to use counter-deception to defend themselves and expose his treachery. They had little choice.

"I'll do it," she stated.

Agent Fauchard had been placed in charge of the fire team sent to scout the parallel world that the guys back in the lab had dubbed "Svartalfheim" after the so-called dark elves of Norse mythology. Parts of it abutted the Other or bled into its boundaries, but it seemed to be a different dimension entirely.

The sky overhead was curiously low and cloaked with dark, oppressive clouds, a weird and disturbing contrast with the dry, desiccated landscape. The ground beneath their feet was composed mostly of reddish rock and dust, and there was little vegetation save bleached-looking thorny vines and the occasional cluster of dead trees.

Oddly-carven boulders or rock ridges eroded by the wind added to the alien nature of the terrain.

"Okay," Fauchard spoke into his intercom, and his words were beamed across the astral plane and back to HQ. "We've successfully arrived. All quiet on the western front except for the scanner. According to it, we're standing in the middle of a gigantic swarm of colorful dots."

One of the three men with him snickered at that, then stopped himself.

Fauchard ignored him as he readjusted his gas mask and hoisted his arcanoplasm rifle. He and one other man had standard plasma guns, which did arcane-elemental damage to physical targets. The other two had dispersal rifles, which were essentially the opposite: they weakened and dissolved the arcane structures of incorporeal entities, though tests had found that they could do some damage to living things too.

In any event, combat was not the goal. Theirs was strictly a recon mission.

Agent Velasquez, supervising the operation from back at headquarters, watched the scanner screen in his office while speaking into a microphone. The big screen was subdivided into eight sections, one for each of the worlds or regions currently being investigated by a patrol.

"Advance, but carefully," he instructed them. "Keep adjusting your visors if you don't see anything. Abominations from different planes of existence may only be visible on the right infrared or ultraviolet frequencies."

"Roger," Fauchard acknowledged him. "Move out."

The four agents moved quickly and quietly across the

rusty earth, darting from one random object or obstacle to another and keeping out of sight as much as possible. Gusts of wind picked up now and again, filling the air with red dust and obscuring their transmissions with static.

"Hey," one of the men whispered and pointed toward a barely-elevated small plane of rock with a yawning black mouth. "Cave."

Fauchard noted the information and glanced around, seeing two other entrances in distant parts of the rusty stone. He checked his scanner. Masses of dots were still moving around, seemingly on top of them.

Not on top, he realized—below.

"Right," he said to HQ, "the dark elves are using underground tunnels and caverns to reposition themselves under our feet. Judging by the number of blips on our screen, I'd say they have a colony down there the size of Tucson or so. We're going up to one of the cave mouths and looking in."

"Hey," Velasquez replied into the intercom, "*cautious-like*, okay? Retreat the goddamn *second* you even think they might be after you."

The nearest hole in the ground, framed by drooping spikes of red rock, loomed closer. Something started beeping; it was Fauchard's team's scanner, warning them of supernatural beings getting closer.

"Whoa," the fire team leader quipped. "We, uh, may have a problem. Preparing to pack up and…shit. *Shit!*"

The colored blobs on the screen rushed out in a solid wave, then the screen went dark. No sound came from the intercom.

The senior agent in the office barked, "Fauchard. Respond, Fauchard! What the fuck?"

Two more screens went black, too. Technicians fiddled with knobs.

"Well, damn," Velasquez snapped. "What the hell happened to them? Is anyone showing technical difficulties with the transmission?

Someone did a quick check on his device. "No, sir. Unless it's entirely on their end, which is, uhh, possible..."

His tone indicated that he was just saying that to be diplomatic. They all knew Fauchard and his men were dead.

The senior agent resisted the urge to kick chairs, flip laptops off of desks onto the floor, and pick up garbage cans to hurl them at walls. Instead, he asked his cohorts, "Does anyone know what to make of this? Before I offer my professional opinion, naturally."

No one did. Half of them shrugged, and of the other half, most offered only vague, meaningless commentary meant to fill uncomfortable silences with sound. Two made doom-and-gloom pronouncements that everyone tried to ignore.

"Dammit," Velasquez snarled. "As bad as this looked to begin with, it's an order of magnitude worse if we can't even get word back to check on our troops who've gone missing in action. The boys at the top of the totem pole aren't hesitating for once to declare this a maximum alert situation. And why don't we have word from fucking Bailey? I mean, we left a message at her house and a voicemail."

It annoyed and embarrassed him to consider that they

leaned on her for support, but she was a goddess. That could not be overlooked.

He made the decision to pull the other teams back. Losing them all would be a minor disaster and terrible for morale. Plus, they needed every available agent ready to fight. The scanners didn't always tell them things in ways they could understand, but they didn't lie, either.

Right now, the scanners were indicating a full-scale *invasion* of paranormal and otherworldly creatures.

Velasquez called his superiors and conveyed the information and hunches to them. "We haven't yet gotten confirmation on any of the blips. Three of our teams went dark and the remaining ones aren't seeing anything yet, so I'm pulling them back for the sake of personnel retention. I repeat, *invasion-level numbers* are moving toward us. Is there something we should know about, something that we missed? Like an ancient prophecy or some shit? I hate those things. Whatever the case, sirs, everything else in the world is secondary unless this turns out to be a goodwill mission by a bunch of sex angels or something, and when has *that* ever happened?"

A few of the men laughed, but nervous strain underlay their voices.

Velasquez was well aware that his people needed a confidence boost, and sooner rather than later.

Dammit, Bailey! he thought. *Why aren't you here, fraternizing with the troops? Be a good goddess and move your ass.*

Footsteps approached behind them, and Velasquez turned.

It was Townsend, walking with the aid of a cane,

looking older and paler than his former understudy recalled, but otherwise like his old self again.

The room cheered.

Townsend waved with a smile, but it was replaced by his standard grimace after a second or two. "Hi," he said. "Looks like you're having some trouble."

"All right," Loki concluded. "Now to enact, ah, Phase One, as you people would put it. Simply call Fenris and have him come to you. Say it's urgent."

Bailey wasn't so sure. "You're putting a lot of faith in my acting skills, you know."

Loki shrugged. "Yes, but you've proven to be an excellent thespian so far. We know you won't let us down. Tell Fenris what happened. Not all the details, natch, or that you understand what's going on, but enough for him not to question your motives or reasons for being here. Show him the devastation, the bodies, the trail. Say you're looking for Balder out of pure concern for his safety but haven't found him yet."

Bailey inquired, "Yeah, and then what? What if he gets suspicious, or what if he knows you came and talked to me right before I called him?"

Loki shrugged. "Oh, he won't. Probably. And if he does, you're smart enough to figure it out, aren't you? All speculation aside, I anticipate that he'll come to you of his own volition once you inform him of the situation. Leaping to your aid, or so it seems, and also seizing the chance to spirit you into battle against the forces he has gone out of his way to assemble. Like he did not long ago, remember?"

She did. Together they'd slain small armies of frost trolls and platoons of dark elves. She still didn't understand how this could be. How could Fenris be working with the monstrous species while participating in the slaughter of their warriors? Loki had explained the politics of it, but it made no emotional sense to her.

The god of mischief finished up his spiel. "I believe that Fenris will stoop even to betraying his allies in the course of achieving his aims. He'll happily sacrifice them for the sake of powering you up and then sacrificing you, allowing him to survive and reign beyond the end of the universe. So, if you would, please call him. Balder and I will take our leave."

The girl agreed. She couldn't think of a better plan. If nothing else, she'd be able to see how Fenris reacted to the news of Balder's injury and go from there.

Loki helped Balder to his feet, and the pair took their leave through the portal the mischief-lord had come through. The purple light of the doorway winked out.

Bailey stood alone in the thick, shadowy forest. Daylight was waning; it would be pitch black soon. She inhaled slowly and raised her arms, sending out streamers of her divine and arcane consciousness toward her would-be mentor, the wolf-father.

"Fenris," she intoned. Then, louder, "*Fenris!* I have need of you. Come forth, god of werewolves. Aid me! Manifest!"

She imbued her words with magic and sent them echoing throughout the dimensions of the known universe. She could not recall if the incantation was correct, but it ought to be close enough. He usually heard her when she called for him.

The astral reverberations fell still and quiet, and there was no sound in the forest at first, except for the slow beating of Bailey's heart.

Then a glimmering amethyst-hued doorway opened in the air to her side, much like the one Loki had used. Out of it stepped his son.

Fenris looked at her. As usual, his face was mostly veiled by his hood, but she noted that the tilt of his head and the subtle twist of his mouth suggested he was more perplexed than anything.

"Bailey," he began, "what is the matter? I have been busy patrolling the borders of Asgard against any attempts by the monstrous people to breach their treaties with us. Is it something serious?"

It pained her to realize that if it hadn't been for all the evidence she'd heard previously, she would at this moment have no reason to suspect Fenris of lying to her.

"Yeah," she replied, "pretty damn serious. I came here looking to see if Carl wanted to help out with some stuff and to touch base with everyone, but the castle had been attacked, and everyone but five people had been wiped out."

She relayed the tale of what happened, keeping most of the details accurate though a tad vague. Obviously, she left out the parts involving Loki and Balder.

The wolf-god grimaced in a way that was moody and severe even for him.

"It comes as no shock. I had feared something like this might happen since there is unrest all across the dimensional boundaries. We foolishly assumed that the training grounds would be safe due to the presence of so many demigod-level beings and the constant presence of skilled guards and trainers, but it wasn't sufficient. Come, we must halt the dark elves' invasion. They are moving on many fronts. I was preparing to inform you."

Though Bailey had half-anticipated this—Loki had said to expect as much—somehow the idea that the elves were attacking multiple places simultaneously came as a mild shock.

And that was only the dark *alfar*. What, she wondered, were all the other monstrous species up to?

"Goddammit, I thought we'd negotiated a settlement or a ceasefire with them. What the hell is happening to the world lately?"

Fenris' answer was ominous. "*That* will remain to be seen. In this specific case, the dark elves are making a massive push against us. They've congregated in numbers too great for most to resist. There is no guarantee that we will be able to stop them, but we must try. Come, and we will begin to retaliate against them. Be careful, Bailey, but don't hold back, either. This might be the biggest conflict we've yet been involved in."

She nodded. "We'll do whatever we have to do to protect the realms. I'm with you."

The tall man smiled and turned away from her to dismiss the portal he'd entered by and conjure a new one in its place. He seemed relaxed.

I think I've succeeded in convincing him I've got his back. He doesn't suspect me. I hope. But let's see how he reacts to a little something else.

"Oh, also," she remarked as Fenris opened the gateway, "I was looking for Balder. I ran into him briefly. He was wounded with a magic arrow or something and told me to leave him be. He went back to Asgard, I think, to have the other gods remove it. He was pretty messed up. Seemed confident he'd be okay, but I'm worried."

Fenris stiffened, and he did not reply immediately. He turned around.

"Balder was attacked as well?" he mused. "That is disturbing. I fear for him too, since there are accursed arrows in the universe that can cause tremendous harm to gods as well as lower beings. Do you have any leads, any evidence as to who or what might be responsible?"

She shook her head. "Nope. Aside from the dark elves being all over this forest, naturally. I don't know anything beyond that."

"Well," said the wolf-father, "if Balder is returning home, he will get the help he needs and likely survive. Now, follow me." He stepped through the portal.

But, Bailey speculated, *how much longer will he survive? And what am I walking into?*

CHAPTER SIX

The homeworld of the dark *alfar* was not a pleasant realm. Nothing about it was soft or reassuring. Bailey had been here once before, briefly. It hadn't been high on her list of places to visit again.

It was a desert of red rock and orangish-brown dust, of small jagged mountains and mysterious cavern complexes, with sporadic boulders eroded by the wind and weird petrified trees and vines breaking up the desolate monotony. Overhead, the sky was masked with low, thick clouds the color of slate.

Bailey couldn't recall if this was the exact place she and Fenris had come to on their previous excursion or somewhere else since it all looked pretty similar to her. She asked the were-god.

"No," he said, "this is not the location we came to before. It's closer to the edge of their realm, with some overlap with the Other. Not far, in fact, from the dark forest where you called me. It also seems that your human friends in the Agency sent people here quite recently. And yet..."

There were no signs of human intrusion. No footprints, relics, or the markings of any significant fighting. No bodies, either. It was as though the spot had been undisturbed for decades.

"Huh," Bailey mused. "As if everything wasn't weird enough already."

It was quiet as they advanced toward an area with a greater than average concentration of dark openings to the underground, but it wasn't long before a low noise combined with a rising vibration brought them both to a halt.

They stood, neither moving nor breathing. They only listened.

The ground was rumbling. So many bodies were moving around beneath them within the bowels of the rock that it qualified as a seismic event, a minor earthquake.

"Uh," Bailey piped up, in a louder voice, "we have a problem here, Fenris."

"I know," he growled.

From the cave mouths all around them streamed black-armored, white-haired archers and swordsmen, their collective hissing battle cry like the descent of a giant tidal wave toward a hapless shore—hundreds of them, with hundreds and thousands more streaming out behind them. The earth emptied itself of their numberless horde.

Bailey punched the ground, conjuring an expanding semicircular wave of water that grew in size and power, becoming a tidal wave that smashed into the first of their foes. It drove them back in rolling heaps, washing them away.

She pushed the torrential waters toward a cluster of cave openings and then froze it, trapping dozens of *alfar* within the ice and blocking a paltry few of their points of egress to the surface.

But more were coming, not only from other caves but from hidden places aboveground. Forty at a time leaped down from a low, jagged line of cliffs and hills, while scouts and sentries sprouted from behind what looked like every single tree, rock, and bush across the visible landscape.

Fenris retaliated with huge gales of wind and by seizing the rock beneath their feet in sheets an acre wide, turning the ground itself over like a revolving trash can lid and dumping elves back into the subterranean depths from which they'd come.

They screamed and growled and arrows from their bows blanketed the sky, colliding uselessly with the two deities' hastily-conjured shields.

But for every dozen they forced away, incapacitated, or destroyed, another three dozen rushed to meet them.

"Bailey," Fenris shouted, "we can't win here. Not now, not without serious and needless risk. We must flee and get reinforcements!" He shifted into his hulking house-sized wolf form and stomped on elves, flung them aside, and batted groups across the stony plain.

The werewitch created a field of static electricity a quarter-mile across. Fifty or so elves ran into it and froze, their muscles seizing. It wouldn't kill them, but it would hold them off for a bit.

"No objections here!" she yelled. "We need to clear a place to warp out, though!"

She selected a spot off to her right that seemed less dense with adversaries than anywhere else in the wasteland and detonated an expanding wave of concussive force. Elves flew head over heels through the air or were driven straight back, leaving a broad circle empty of them.

Fenris and Bailey bounded into the cleared zone. The wolf-father was more experienced at conjuring portals, so he worked on that while Bailey surrounded the two of them with a dome-shield. A thousand furious *alfar* crashed into it, gnashing their teeth and waving their scimitars.

A purple doorway appeared at the center of the safe zone. Fenris, back in human form, made a sharp beckoning motion and plunged into the astral murk. Bailey gave one last glance at the army they'd failed to defeat before she followed him out of their domain.

Bailey stumbled through the portal, more disoriented than was the norm for her, and the recession of the dizzying cold left her staggered in the grass of her backyard. They had landed a short way behind the pole barn, at the edge of the Nordin family property before it ascended into the forested slopes of the Cascade foothills.

It was dark; she guessed close to midnight. She'd left Earth at dusk. It had been afternoon at the training grounds, so that combined with the differential passage of time in the Other had disoriented her.

Fenris leaned over her to close the gateway the instant

she was clear of it. "They don't possess the magic to follow us," he pointed out. "But they know the longer route to our worlds. It's only a matter of time until we have to deal with *all* of them."

"I don't doubt it anymore," Bailey muttered.

Mentally, she added, *Because you riled them up.*

They turned toward her home, walking past the pole barn, and the girl watched and listened. Half the lights in the house were on, and she could clearly hear the sounds of many people moving about and talking. It was as though her brothers had decided to throw a party. It didn't seem too festive, though. She suspected it was another war council of local Weres.

As the pair strode toward the back door, the girl thought of something.

I told my brothers about the situation with Fenris, but how much did they tell other people? Do they have any way of knowing that we need to play along for now? All it takes is one moron to get huffy and wonder what Fenris is doing here, given what we know about him, then the entire plan is down the shitter.

She turned to the wolf-father and put her hand on his arm. "Fenris, could you wait here a sec? I want to assure everyone I'm okay and kinda ease them into what's going on. No offense, but usually when you're around, that means there's trouble."

His jaw tightened for a split second, but he nodded. "I understand, but we don't have much time to waste. Please hurry."

The werewitch rushed ahead, pulling open the back door and intruding upon a group of over two dozen people who'd filled the kitchen, dining room, halls, and living room. She also saw and heard signs of more folks out in the front yard.

Jacob, sitting at the head of the dining table, waved to her. "Bailey! Hey, we just got some people together to talk about what we'll do if we have to fight against—"

"Yes," she shouted, her voice loud and sharp, cutting him off. "That's great, thanks. We can use all the friends we can get."

She glared sharply at her brother and everyone else present, raising a finger to her lips and pointing surreptitiously behind her with her other hand.

She added, "Yeah, fighting the monster invasions from all these fucking parallel worlds. Me and Fenris beat up a lot of them a couple weeks back, but it wasn't enough. Now there's a whole horde of the sons of bitches headed straight for Earth. That's what I came to talk about, but it looks like you are way ahead of me. I see plenty of familiar faces."

Her brothers had summoned several of the strongest and most prominent pack alphas, as well as their lieutenants and other respected fighters, from amongst the Weres of the Hearth Valley, plus from some packs farther afield. All were men who'd been with her before and during the war against the Venatori. In particular, she noted Will Waldsbach, who'd been her strongest supporter among the lycanthropic community besides her own family.

She glanced aside, looking through the dining room's doorway into the living area in time to see her fiancé stride in, with Dante and Charlene trailing behind and beside him.

"Ah," Roland greeted her, "there you are. We were just discussing whether to try looking for you, calling you, or praying to you. How did things go?"

She frowned. "Could've been better. Was I gone for only a few hours or a whole day or more?"

Dante, a wizard not dissimilar from Roland though perhaps three or four years younger, raised a finger. "Twenty-seven hours, almost exactly," he observed. "If it had been three, we Seattleites wouldn't have made it here in time."

"Right," she muttered. "Good point. Okay, well, Fenris is here to help out and explain to everyone what the current situation is, and then we'll take volunteers. There's a battle coming, and it's better if we fight it sooner rather than later. On *their* turf. We've done enough fighting in this town."

Some of the assembled witches and werewolves looked confused, and Bailey knew why. They didn't understand why Fenris was suddenly their friend again. She gave them sharp looks and repeated her pantomimed motion to stay silent.

Then she leaned out the back door and motioned for the wolf-father to come in.

The tall, broad-shouldered man in the hooded coat greeted them only briefly before he set to summarizing the looming threat of the dark elves' invasion. Pleasantries had never been his strongest suit.

While he spoke, Bailey examined the team her friends

had assembled, and she was impressed. Numbers-wise, they were as nothing compared to droves of dark *alfar* she'd escaped, but fifty or so committed and powerful individuals were nothing to scoff at. In addition to the various Weres, Roland and Dante had also summoned a number of talented witches, whose extensive magical abilities Bailey could sense.

Since she'd ascended to godhood, the arcane gave off a smell that never went away.

Fenris told them all, "We are facing a scenario of total war—a full invasion by an entire race, not merely an organization, as was the case with the Venatori. The numbers of the dark *alfar* make those of the sorceresses' Order look insignificant in contrast. We must move quickly and retaliate with immediate and overwhelming force. There can be no holding back, no hesitation, no fighting at anything less than your full ability, yet we have to be disciplined, organized. Bailey and I will go over an outline of our general strategy, and I will take us to a place where we can use the terrain and a modicum of good timing and good luck to our advantage."

They went over the tactics they would employ. It was impossible to plan for everything, but it helped that most of the people present had experience in battle.

Everyone agreed that Bailey and Fenris, as deities who were orders of magnitude stronger than the rest of them, would be on the front lines, acting as the artillery and doing as much damage to the dark elves as they could.

The witches and wizards would offer both offensive and defensive support, while the Weres would be divided between bodyguards for the casters and highly mobile search-and-destroy teams who could pursue and eliminate small bands of elves who tried to flee or reposition them-selves for better archery. The Were teams would return to the main group before they could be cut off and encircled by other swarms of the enemy.

The core group departed the house, bringing along their hangers-on from the front yard, with everyone gathering out back, where there was more room. Fenris opened an unusually wide portal, big enough for three people to pass through at once, and Bailey gave the troops one final, brief pep talk.

"Keep in mind," she announced, "this is no cakewalk, and pretending like it is won't do us any good. We will be in danger. Fenris and I had to retreat, but we didn't know what to expect. Now we do, and having you people with us will make a world of difference. I've met most of you, and I trust you. I couldn't possibly ask for better backup. We can do this."

Four or five people made encouraging comments, and others pumped fists in the air.

Fenris turned to them before leading the way through the gate. "Remember, we cannot defeat all of them, but we can divide them, pick off many of their best troops, and most importantly, engage and eliminate their king. He must be our main target." He turned to the shimmering violet surface and concluded with, "Follow me," before stepping in.

Bailey was right behind him, and Roland behind her. The dozens of Weres and witches filed in next, the whole group spinning through the astral channels in an instant before emerging into the red waste of the *alfar*'s home plane.

At first glance, the werewitch grasped that they'd come to a different point than the one she and Fenris had visited earlier since the elven army had advanced beyond that. The skyline and lay of the land, though similar, were not identical.

She also grasped that they had about ten seconds before the thousands-strong horde came within closing distance of combat. The entire ground for what looked like a square mile was covered with black-armored, white-haired forms.

Someone behind her exclaimed, "Holy living fuck!"

Bailey raised her right arm. "Shields up! Everyone fall into position like we said!"

She and Fenris stormed forth, leaving the rest of the group behind while Roland and the other witches conjured protective barriers around them. And not a second too soon since the elves immediately began firing arrows from their black bows.

Fenris incinerated the projectiles that came toward him, and Bailey swatted others aside. The remaining ones were trapped in or clattered off of the large amalgamated shield surrounding their allies.

Then the *alfar* shouted in unison, their battle cry a single hissing voice that was like a sandstorm or a torrent of water, and they charged with drawn and waving swords.

In the back of her mind, Bailey admired the creatures' bravery since the ones out front had to know what was in store for them—namely, the wrath of two gods.

She and Fenris hurled waves, bolts, storms, and vortices of arcane and elemental force at the army's vanguard. Colored light flashed, air crackled, and dust and rock formed clouds as the entire front line of the advancing horde was lost to sight and then to existence. Hundreds of *alfar* died at once.

But they were only a fraction of the whole, which Bailey estimated numbered between twelve to fifteen thousand. She doubted this was the entire dark elf force; they likely had multiple other brigades, divisions, and legions elsewhere.

The *alfar* host split down the middle and continued their charge at flanking angles toward the two deities and the small expeditionary group behind them. By now, the witches had begun tossing offensive magic at their foes, picking off many, while most of the Weres had shifted in preparation for melee combat.

Bailey mixed elemental attacks with advancing barrier waves, forcing elves backward while destroying them or hurling large numbers of them into the sky. Fenris had shifted into a giant lupine monster again, and he stomped, thrashed, devoured, and breathed out storms of fire and ice. Noise and chaos were everywhere.

Will Waldsbach led four of his pack fighters in wolf form on a rapid hunter-destroyer mission against a squad of elven archers who'd taken position on a nearby ridge and were launching arrows at the human forces in a continuous wave of suppressing fire. They moved fast, nimbly dodging when half the *alfar* changed their attentions to trying to shoot *them*. Hairy quadrupedal bodies feinted, leaped, and twisted through the air, bounding up the ridge.

One wolf took an arrow in the shoulder and yelped, though his early pounce brought down the archer who'd wounded him. The other four piled into the remaining eight elves, knocking some down and biting the legs and clawing the faces of others. In ten seconds, it was over. The snipers lay dead.

As the five lycanthropes hurried back toward the main group, though, the one who'd been injured lagged badly behind. The others slowed their pace to protect him.

Dante was closest to the Were quintet and noticed what was happening. "Oh, crap," he breathed, seeing two dozen *alfar* swordsmen advancing down a nearby slope toward the group.

He threw out his hand and conjured a wall of arcane shield-matter a couple of yards in front of the elves. They crashed into it, stumbling and disoriented, and it took them a moment to grasp what had happened and go around the translucent wall's edges. By then, Will and his followers had covered enough distance to reach the safety of the main force.

Will shifted back to human form. "Healer! We need someone with healing magic experience!" he shouted.

Roland had been busy blocking arrows and casting exploding fireballs toward groups of elves who tried to sneak around Bailey and Fenris, but, sighing, he paused and ran back to the South Cliff alpha, instantly taking in what had happened and infusing the wounded lycanthrope with curative energy.

"There," the wizard reassured him. "You won't be able to fight or run at full potential, but that ought to take care of most of the pain and stop it from getting any worse. Be careful."

He turned back to the main battle, his hands raised and ready.

Bailey and Fenris unleashed artillery-level blasts of arcane plasma, channeling the heat, force, and sonic disturbance away from their allies. The landscape for half a mile flattened, and *alfar* died by the dozens.

The two deities stood front and center in the brief respite-space they'd purchased, while smoke rose, arrows rained down, and bodies dropped around them.

The wolf-father turned to the girl. "We must find their king. Gormyr is his name. Challenge him, defeat him, and take his power! That will neutralize the horde and put us in a better position to confront the next threat."

Bailey inhaled. "Noted." She was of two minds, and it felt strange to her. She knew without any doubt that what Fenris had asked of her would further his own nefarious plans. And yet, it was also the best and smartest thing to do right now. Whatever the bigger picture might hold, she and all her friends would be swamped and killed if they did not find a way to win the battle within a matter of minutes, half an hour at the absolute most.

And retreating would only allow the elves to continue their march toward Asgard and Earth. It was not an option.

She raised a hand, conjuring a beacon of light that blazed above her head, and bellowed, "Onward!"

CHAPTER SEVEN

Bailey's makeshift army had torn through most of the *alfar* division, killing a third of its members and dividing the rest in half. The front portion of their host had retreated into a collection of caves and tunnels, while the remainder of them had fled, at first. Then they'd looped around to harry the mortal forces from behind with arrows and sporadic ambushes from the rocks.

One witch and one werewolf had died. Neither was anyone Bailey knew well, but she had to force herself to stay focused on the all-important task at hand: to plunge ahead and defeat the horde at its source.

Fenris gestured at the nearest large cave mouth. "There. That should lead to the underground system where Gormyr dwells. I can sense him; he's not far. Of course, we can expect that he'll be well protected."

A platoon of archers and swordsmen had appeared ahead, before the dark entrance that the were-god had indicated.

"Yeah," Bailey remarked, "no shit. I'm getting tired of these assholes already, truth be told." She launched a multi-forked lightning bolt at the group, which destroyed some of their arrows and killed or paralyzed them all. Her forward group of wolves finished off the ones who still lived.

At the same instant, though, more elves popped out of a cluster of boulders behind them, sending arrows through a narrow gap in their shields while warriors with blades assaulted the sides of their formation, trying to overwhelm the witches.

When Bailey turned back, her friends had defeated about half of them, but the ambushers were so well mingled with her people that she could not attack all of them at once. She prayed that Roland, Dante, Charlene, and Will knew what they were doing. Meanwhile, the werewitch telekinetically grabbed two elves and dashed them into the nearest rock wall at a good hundred or so miles per hour. Their bodies crumpled, and they did not move again.

The group fought free of the ambush, though another Were and one witch had taken wounds.

Bailey swept her arm over her head. "Into the tunnel! Weres on the outside, witches on the inside. We can finish this right away if we get to their king!"

She allowed Fenris to spearhead the way into the cave. In the back of her mind, she wondered if she could trust him with such an important duty; but he clearly had more knowledge of the *alfar* realm than she did. And his plans called for the two of them to seem to be on the same side until the bitter end of the process. For the time being, she had to play along and hope the hour of his betrayal was still in the future.

Behind Fenris, four Weres piled in, then Bailey went, with Roland and a handful of other witches right behind her. The remainder of the casters followed, with the rest of the Weres bringing up the rear. The witches kept them shielded and also cast spells of gentle illumination to make the rocky tunnels navigable for themselves. The lycanthropes had little trouble seeing in the dark.

Dozens of elves chased them into the corridor from the surface. The rearward casters destroyed them or delayed them with walls of fire or ice or bolts of arcane plasma, and the Weres in the utmost back ripped apart the ones who got too close.

Other combatants came at them from side tunnels. Fenris had led them into a labyrinth, a honeycombed network of subterranean passages, which likely acted as a military base for the entire main force of the *alfar*'s army. Bailey threw sheets and columns of supercharged static electricity down any tunnel where something moved toward them. It would be enough to paralyze or kill any elves it struck without damaging the structural integrity of the corridor.

Fenris led them through winding masses of blackish-red stone, and the tunnel widened enough for Bailey and the wolf-father to fight side by side in front, though the girl continued to divide her attention between that which lay ahead and that which chased them.

One of their wounded Weres slipped outside a faltering

shield, and sword-wielding elves converged on him to finish him off. Snarling, Bailey detonated a flaming explosion that obliterated the *alfar* swordsmen, but too late to save the wolf.

Their path led into a vast, airy, sprawling cavern, across a makeshift bridge of rock that spanned a black chasm below. Other paths between other openings crossed the walls of the pit, and here dark elf archers had taken position to snipe at them.

"Goddammit!" Roland exclaimed. "Can't things get easier instead of harder for once?" He raised strong, towering shields on both sides of the path, and their arrows ricocheted off to plummet into the void below.

The elves trailing behind them launched bolts of their own over and through the middle of the path. One grazed Roland's arm and the wizard faltered, his left-hand shield dissipating.

Bailey spun toward him as another volley of arrows came across the chasm. "No!" She deflected them, barely, then seized telekinetic control of the very rock of the cavern wall, bringing it down on the archers, crushing them and destroying the path. The ruins of both tumbled into the darkness.

She turned to the other side, where another group of bowmen was approaching from a closer, broader tunnel. The girl dislodged more stone within the corridor's walls and slammed both halves together, closing the passage off and reducing the *alfar* within to paste.

Then they ran ahead, reentering an enclosed area and clashing with a squad of swordsmen. Bailey pulled free her blade, noting the way Fenris looked at it curiously, and the two of them cut down the warriors in seconds.

Not far beyond lay an archway, beyond which was another dome-like cavern, albeit one which seemed to have a solid floor. Forty elves burst out, firing a volley of arrows before charging with their scimitars.

The wolf-father blocked the projectiles while Bailey used her sword to throw a wave of freezing gas into the front lines of the platoon, killing the first dozen and leaving their ice-statue corpses to obstruct the ones behind.

Fenris gestured at the space ahead with a big, clenching hand. "This is not Gormyr's main throne room, but I strongly suspect he's here. It's a forward command center, which will allow him to stay close to his troops while on this side of their realm but remain in a secure location at the same time. Move!"

"Gotcha," Bailey replied, throwing a percussive shock-wave into a cluster of guards who streamed out of the archway toward them. The frozen ones shattered and the others staggered into the walls. "There's got to be *something* important here if they're fighting to defend it so goddamn hard."

They plunged into the warriors who remained stand-ing, blasting them into the cave walls or cutting them down, bulling their way into the chamber beyond. At once, they found themselves facing down two dozen elves who could only be an elite honor guard.

Bailey paused for a brief instant. The new adversaries wore shining golden armor and deep purple robes, and they carried glaive-like bladed staffs as well as short swords at their sides. Something about the way the armor glowed faintly suggested that it offered the wearers significant protection against magic. She couldn't be sure, but the hunch was strong.

Fenris barked, "Plunge through! We'll handle them."

Bailey threw a net of crackling lightning at the praetorians, but it did no more than spark against their helmets, pauldrons, and breastplates and momentarily slow them. "Shit," she muttered, then dashed forward, surrounding herself with a battering ram's worth of arcane shield.

She struck one of the elite guards head-on. His glaive glanced off her shield, and he was thrown off-balance to clatter aside. Another tried to stab her from the side and she ducked the blow, driving her sword deep into his armpit before ripping it free.

Then she was past them, as Fenris and her friends engaged the others. She ran forward on a broad open stone floor toward an elevated platform where a distinctive figure sat on a small, portable throne.

He did not look much different from the others, though he was taller than most, with a bearing that was less feral and more aloof and haughty. His long silver hair was tied into a braid that fell behind his shoulders, and a slim black crown encircled his brow. The gold-hued armor he wore was similar to that of his bodyguards, though limited to leg greaves, shoulder pauldrons, and a vest of scales, rather than full heavy plate. He wore a black cape and a scimitar at his side that was slightly longer and more finely-decorated than that of the average warrior.

He looked down his nose at the girl. "You. So soon."

Behind Bailey, the struggle against the elite guards had reached a stalemate, and Fenris shoved his way past the rest of them to stand at the werewitch's elbow and point up the dais at the monarch.

The two men locked eyes. Gormyr's smirk faded when Fenris spoke.

"Your reign is over," the wolf-god boomed. "You have broken the non-aggression pact we had made, foully betraying us by moving your entire army toward the boundaries that lead to Asgard and Earth. Our realms will be spared the surging numbers of your blood-maddened people, and you will cease to live."

The pompous elven face fell in deep dismay. Bailey noticed that the ruler was not looking at her but staring at Fenris.

Holding her bright sword in two hands, the girl held it up and aimed the point toward the elf's face. "Gormyr, King of the Dark *Alfar*, I, Bailey Nordin, hereby challenge you to single combat for control of your army."

He turned his face back to her and spread his bony hands. "I know of you, Bailey Nordin, and I had expected us to meet, although not as soon as this. Treachery must be afoot."

He allowed the bitterness of his last statement to hang in the air for a moment before resuming his spiel.

"But it makes no difference, just as it is unimportant that you are officially a goddess. For you are a neophyte, an amateur, barely able to control your powers, whereas I am heir to eons upon eons of elite training as both a swordsman and a sorcerer. And furthermore, woman-child, your death is inevitable, for it is written into the prophecies that underlie our current situation. You cannot fight Fate. You can only fight *me*...and fail."

Bailey's nostrils flared. "Well, you're half right. Bring it on, and let's see about the rest."

Gormyr walked steadily forward and raised his sword in a slow, smooth motion, settling into a fighting stance, the blade in a high defensive guard. "Control of my army, you say?"

"Yes," she shot back. "If I win, leadership over the dark elves passes to me."

The monarch laughed drily. "If you win, Bailey, they will fall upon you and destroy you, sweeping you aside and battening the walls of Asgard until either they fall at last or the final elf dies. You cannot stop what's been set in motion."

She trembled in frustration. "Fight me! Quit talking."

Behind and around her, the *alfar* who'd been chasing them had piled into the chamber and stood watching, tense and ready.

"As you wish," Gormyr said. He looked slowly at Fenris, his face grim, and the two men locked eyes for the span of three heartbeats before the king turned his gaze back to the werewitch.

The *alfar* blade leapt from its wielder's hand with such nimble speed that Bailey was shocked and only narrowly avoided taking its point in her eyes. She flung her head back, wheeling to the side and swinging her sword upward toward his hand and arm, but he'd already retracted it and was circling around toward her flank.

Bailey feinted a thrust and then slashed powerfully at Gormyr's head while the elf leaned to the side, cutting toward the girl's legs. She jumped twelve feet in the air, seeking to descend and cut her enemy in half from above, overpowering him with sheer force.

He responded by raising his hand and summoning a bolt of lightning from above her. She realized what he was doing at the last fraction of a second and took the bolt on her sword, absorbing the energy and striking toward him as she landed.

The king swept aside the lightning stroke with a mixture of water and arcane shield-matter, then his sword once again drove toward her throat.

Bailey's mind worked like a machine, recalling and employing everything she'd learned about fencing and combat. Her arms and her sword were one, moving with a speed and efficiency of which she was proud. Yet it was scarcely enough to fight the tall monarch to a draw.

There came a brief lull, and Bailey deployed the secret weapon in her arsenal, the one she knew with near-certainty that Gormyr would not expect.

She visualized long tendrils of magic emerging from her to lock into the king's chest and head, piercing him and opening a one-way channel between them. She started draining him of his power, as she'd done before to two goddesses. Since Gormyr was less than a deity, powerful though he was, she knew she could handle it.

The elven monarch did not appear to notice at first. He lunged at her again, and once more she blocked his strike. He was slower than he'd been before, if only minutely.

When he wheeled around for a second slash, he faltered, and his eyes widened.

Bailey swept her blade toward his throat. He dodged it, but he'd grasped that something was wrong. He raised a hand to hurl a blast of magic at her, but the fireball that erupted from his fingers was weak, fading into smoke after only a few yards. Bailey blocked it with ease.

Still she siphoned his power, absorbing most of it into herself and letting the rest bleed into the ground, to be sponged back up by the fabric of the realm itself. A charge went through her like three cups of Russell's coffee.

"No," Gormyr rasped. "*No!*"

He charged at her, stopped to throw a knee-level kinetic shockwave, and then lashed out again. Bailey hadn't expected a feint of this kind and the shockwave knocked her off balance, though not off her feet. The king's sword sliced across her hip. The wound wasn't deep, but it was painful, and blood ran down her leg.

She retaliated faster than he could. The tip of her sword moved under his sword arm and drew up, cutting armpit and pectoral and causing the *alfar* to lose full control of his weapon. Still his power seeped out.

The werewitch swung her sword again, striking the elven blade dead-on and shattering it. Another sweep of the longsword dug partway into the armor of his midsection, not cutting through it, but denting it inward and gouging the king's abdomen.

Gormyr faltered, a tremor going through his lithe body, and fell to one knee, barely able to brace himself on his broken sword. His face was contorted in pain and shock, and still his latent magical potential flowed out of the space his body occupied into that of the goddess of Weres and witches.

Feet began to move in a rush, and shadows flickered. The quality of the air and light changed as vast numbers turned and ran. The dark elves abandoned the hall and its surrounding system of tunnels, knowing their king was beaten.

Bailey looked Gormyr in the eyes. "I'll hold you to your bargain."

He tried to laugh and coughed up a spot of blood. "I will be in no position to enforce it, will I? Hold *them* to it. If you can."

The emptying of the chamber continued. *Alfar* fled, yelling and conversing in their sibilant voices, probably arguing whether to obey Bailey as their new leader or to regroup and mount a resistance against her later.

The girl held the point of her sword in front of the elven king's chest, then, with a quick thrust, skewered him through the heart. His eyes squeezed shut as his facial muscles tightened and the breath rattled out of his lungs. Then he slumped over and was still.

Fenris, with a borderline sarcastic tone that was unusual for him, announced, "All hail Bailey Nordin, Queen of the Dark Elves. And we, her agents and ministers."

Cheers, grunts, and shouts of "Yeah!" went around the cavern as her friends and supporters pumped fists in the air.

For her part, the girl breathed deeply, turning her mind to the power she'd absorbed. Gaining so much of it so quickly was always a difficult experience. It was like speeding up a winding road in a car. Exhilarating at first, but there came a moment when you realized you were going too fast, that things might slip out of control, and a nervous, twitchy incoherence threatened to overwhelm the mind.

But she'd dealt with it before, and after a minute or two, she was calm enough to turn to them and speak.

"It's done," she began. "I have no idea if the elves will fight now that he's dead. We'll cross that bridge when we come to it. They might splinter into different groups who can't agree on anything if we're lucky, but they're scattering. We broke their will to fight; they ain't gonna invade Earth anytime right away. I'll call that good enough until further notice. Of course, we couldn't have done this without each other. Thank you, all of you, for fighting so bravely."

After another brief round of celebration, during which she and Roland locked eyes for a much-needed tender moment, Fenris stepped up and raised his arms.

"I must depart," he told them, "to do further scouting and reconnaissance in other realms, where more trouble may be brewing. I will report back to you when I've learned enough. It would be better for the rest of you if you returned to Earth to rest and recover your strength. We may need it."

The wolf-god opened another broad portal back to their realm, then stepped aside and opened a second one only big enough for one person. Bailey nodded to him, watching him leave. She contemplated dashing in after him before he could close it from the other end to discover what the hell he'd be up to next.

No, she ordered herself, *not yet. Soon, the time will be right. But until then, patience.*

Clenching and unclenching her fists, she followed her people through the large gateway, back to Oregon, back home.

CHAPTER EIGHT

The bloodstained forest seemed heavier with silence than usual as Fenris approached the shallow depression next to which his chess table had been set up. Carl was sitting there, waiting for his master. Their eyes met, and the wolf-god beckoned for him to stand.

The scion rose to his feet. "I have located Balder," he stated. A charge of excitement went through him. He nearly trembled with a mixture of nervous energy and combative eagerness.

"Good," said Fenris. "Tell me everything so that we may decide what to do next."

Carl's dark eyes gleamed with triumph. "His arcane energy signature is coming from one of your hunters' forests. I forget the name of it, pardon me. One of the more humanoid-friendly ones, with the paths and signs, But it's under your purview. Balder is there and radiating strongly. I do believe he's *trying* to attract attention to himself, probably in an effort to get the other Asgardians to find him and come to his aid."

"Ah," the wolf-god murmured, "I see. He is not dead yet, then."

His apprentice's face fell by a small margin, detecting the slight note of disappointment in his master's tone.

"He is alive, my lord," Carl went on, "but badly weakened. The accursed arrow is doing its work with slow but deliberate effectiveness. There is a chance he'll be rescued. Shall I depart and finish him off? I've sensed nothing to indicate that there would be any witnesses nearby."

Fenris rubbed his square, stubbled chin. "No. I will deal with him myself. He won't pose much of a challenge in his current state, and I relish the opportunity to deliver the final blow. I've not hunted such prey for far too long."

The scion's eyes dimmed in obvious disappointment, but his only reply was, "Yes, wolf-father, as you wish. May I ask what's been going on in the meantime?"

"All is well," Fenris answered him. "We confronted the dark *alfar*, and Bailey has slain King Gormyr and absorbed his powers." At this point, his barely-contained excitement was palpable. His eyes glimmered beneath his hood. "She is close, Carl, so terribly close to being a proper replacement for me. Furthermore, the elves are now under my command. Bereft of a leader, they will follow me before they follow Bailey, and at my insistence, will attack Asgard in secret, weakening the barrier between the realms. And then, at last, will come the surge which overthrows the divine realm's tyranny once and for all."

Carl chuckled. "Me being only half-divine, I never would have been allowed to reign alongside them. They deserve everything that's coming to them."

"Yes." Fenris beckoned. "Come with me. Though I insist

on delivering the coup de grace to Balder myself, I want you to be present and watch. Consider it your reward for having brought him to this pass."

The scion beamed. "Why, thank you, good sir."

Turning to the side, the wolf-god opened a portal to the realm his apprentice had mentioned. He knew the description, and by sending out his astral consciousness, he easily confirmed Carl's words by picking up the energy signature of the Norse god of beauty. He placed the gateway near enough to Balder that they would find each other without delay, but Fenris and Carl would still have a moment or two to prepare.

Fenris stepped through, followed by the scion. They emerged into another forest, vastly different from the one they'd departed.

Here, groundcover was minimal, and dirt paths wound between the huge, thick, twisted old trees, many of which rose more than a hundred feet. Earth and bark were a rich, deep brown, and the leaves were as bright as emeralds. The sky was overcast though it was a light, almost silvery color, giving the whole place a vital yet somber atmosphere. In places where the trees weren't as thick, grass or flowering bushes grew.

Signs were posted at the junctions of the various footpaths—low stone columns with symbols scratched into them, pointing out directions to one place or another, or giving indications to hunters about where their prey might be located.

The forest was well-stocked with game. Deer and hares frolicked and gamboled. Fenris felt a mild urge to shift and chase them down, more for the thrill of the hunt than for food as he seldom needed to eat.

But he was here on other business.

The throb of intensely concentrated divine energy within the realm was not difficult to locate. Mere seconds after it revealed itself, Fenris heard the sounds of his target, besides.

Feet stumbled in the irregular motions of a man losing his sense and coordination. Branches and leaves rustled, and Balder, not yet visible to the eye, spoke his challenge.

"*Fenris!*" the voice cried. It would once have been a clear, fair voice like the note of a well-honed trumpet, but now it was strained with anguish, emotion, and exhaustion. "Come forth! Face me, you bastard! This realm falls under your dominion. Show yourself!"

The tall man grinned within his hood, his teeth more like a wolf's than a human's. He sensed Carl's satisfaction as well. Balder was badly frazzled, his self-control poor, his emotions raging. It would not be difficult to complete the task of removing him from the pantheon permanently.

The pair moved silently toward the growing noise, and the voice shouted again.

"I know, Fenris!" Heavy breathing, a soft whimper of pain. "I know your plans, you miserable traitor! You turned my students against me. You plotted the whole attack on the training grounds. And I know that you are behind all the unrest lately. You're trying to bring about Ragnarök! Face me, damn you, and answer the charges!"

Fenris and Carl advanced a little farther, allowing themselves to make enough sound to be heard, and the former let his energy signature radiate strongly enough for another deity to sense.

They waited at the edge of a glade until Balder stumbled into it. Carl hung back, hiding behind a tree, while Fenris made no effort to conceal himself. Balder's eyes were wild, his golden hair flying about his shoulders in tangled locks, and dried ichor stained his shoulder and arm.

The god of werewolves took a single slow, heavy step forward.

"Yes," he rumbled, "I *am* responsible for all of that. I am guilty of every charge you've laid before me. Everything you've mentioned happened *because I did it*. All of it. No one else will know, of course, but I want *you* to know in these, your final minutes of existence. You were among the few gods who could pose a legitimate threat to me. But look at you now—wounded, weakened, growing desperate as you succumb to delirium. A shadow of your former self. I will kill you, Balder. You have no chance to save yourself at this point. I've already blocked off any route of escape you might take."

He watched the strained, beautiful face of the injured god grow pale, the eyes bulging in horror as the truth of the wolf-father's words sank in.

"With you dead, that leaves but two who could challenge me. Thor is one, but in truth, his chances are less than yours. I haven't much fear of him. He will be dead soon, and whatever husk of him remains will join you in the abyss. That leaves only Tyr, and by the time the Lord of Justice realizes what is occurring, it will be too late. Goodbye, Balder."

The lord of beauty and innocence produced his sword, the shining rapier blade coming up too slowly to intercept the hulking, towering monstrosity that suddenly bore down on him. A bellowing howl shook the leaves of the trees and the huge furry paw of the dark shape lashed out, its knuckles striking Balder's torso and smashing him into a tree.

Balder shouted in pain and rage, summoning not only the reserves of strength he still possessed but drawing power and vitality from the earth around him. Though it was one of Fenris' domains, the raw stuff of its existence was a kind of life-giving ether that any being of sufficient magical talent could use.

The two gods met each other next on equal footing. Fenris, his wolf form many times the mass of the human-sized Balder, was poised to smash the other into the ground, where his fanged and slavering jaws could complete the task.

But the blond god's strength was far greater than his dimensions would suggest. With his left hand, he stayed the next blow from Fenris' paw, while his right hand lashed out with the sword and drew blood from the dark-furred breast of the giant wolf.

Fenris growled thunderously and clenched his jaws on the blade, flinging it from his foe's grasp and nearly snapping the bones of Balder's arm.

The deity of innocence did not give up. His battle cry had taken on a strangled, desperate note, and tears streamed down his face as he tried to pummel the wolf-beast with his bare hands. Fenris drove him back against the same tree where he'd been flung seconds earlier and brought his head down to bite him in half.

Balder rolled aside and, springing to his feet with agonized effort, found himself face to face with his supposed apprentice.

"Carl," he gasped, "help me. Fenris is a traitor. We must—"

"Oh," the scion remarked as the lycanthropic monstrosity loomed across from him, "I'm well aware of *that*, Balder." He smiled.

Carl's foot plunged forward, striking Balder in the chest and driving him back into the grasping claws of the were-god. The look of horror and emotional pain on the blond god's face had to be genuine, the scion realized. Whatever else he might have figured out, he'd been in the dark about Carl's deception.

Balder tried to spin and stab upward into the massive wolf, but Fenris' jaws came down on his neck, chest, and shoulder, biting deeply, while his claws held the man's arms at bay. Balder screamed, and Fenris flung him aside to crumple against a mass of mossy roots.

The golden deity's form became insubstantial, ghostly, like a cold mist dissipating in the morning sun. The runoff of his divine powers filled the air with a horizontal rain shower of yellow sparks, and what little remained of his body vanished in a flash of light, blue-white tinged with gold. The rushing, tinkling sounds made by his escaping energy subsided. Then nothing remained of him.

Carl burst out laughing, pumping a fist in the air. "Ha-*ha!* You did it, old man, you actually did it. Well, *we* did it, to some extent."

Fenris drew himself up slowly, shifting back into the form of a tall, hooded man, his breaths long and deep. "Correct. Although you should not forget your place as my subordinate, Carl, your efforts were instrumental in all of this. And we are one step closer to Ragnarök. Rejoice! But not for long. We have preparations to make for the next step."

"Oh," the scion remarked, "I am rejoicing." He kept looking at the empty space where Balder, whose apprentice he had pretended to be, had once been. "But, yeah. Let's move on. Plenty more to do."

<hr />

Loki watched. He did not move or speak or breathe or do anything; he only observed the scene playing out in the hunters' forest before him. His son, Fenris, had completed his "killing" of Balder.

Or rather, his destruction of Balder's illusion. Powered by the combined magic of two gods, it was the most convincing level of deception in the universe.

He was hiding behind another illusion, a highly convincing one made from the astral fabric of the realm. Loki had doubled-up the exact view of the woods in this direction and pasted it over reality on a vertical plane in front of where he stood. It served much the same function as a matte painting in a couple of old human movies he'd seen, where a distant landscape was represented by propping the painting up at the edge of the set.

Fenris had not suspected his presence, just as he hadn't

suspected that Balder, in his supposedly final seconds of life, was not truly Balder.

"Alas," the god of mischief sighed, the sound of his voice muffled through magic, "I was expecting something to confound my efforts. That would have made this more of a challenge. And more interesting."

He looked down at his hand, where a tiny light glowed, and with a thought, extinguished it. The point of illumination was the signature of a spell he'd cast to record all that had transpired, creating a perfect holographic representation of the scene that had played out in the clearing.

Everyone would see it. Everyone would hear all that Fenris had arrogantly confessed to, thinking there were no witnesses.

Loki sent the vision to the other gods. It would register in their minds like a vivid memory, implanted there for them to recall at will, and it could still be conjured like a film scene for any mortals who might need to see it, such as Bailey and her friends.

The black-haired deity laughed softly. He still thought of Bailey as a mortal, though she sat on the council of the gods.

Fenris and his treacherous disciple watched the illusion dissipate into nothingness. Since the wolf-lord had defeated the god of innocence with such ease, he did not bother trying to absorb what little remained of his victim's power.

"You know," Loki murmured to no one but himself, "I would have thought that my son would have been...cleverer. He's dumber than I'd expected. Deceit is not his strong point, despite being my child. Oh, his lies have advanced things further than we might have expected, but his plan unravels so easily the instant someone is on to him. Given how heinous his aspirations have become, I suppose it's good that he's this sloppy and foolish, but..." He sighed. "I cannot help but wish for him to have made a better showing. We'll see how he fares when the facades fall and it all goes to brute force. He's rather better at *that*."

The trickster-god secured the playable illusion-scene within himself as he watched Fenris and Carl depart through a portal. Satisfied that they were gone, Loki turned and conjured one of his own, leading back to Greenhearth.

"And now," he murmured, "the girl will have no choice but to believe. I pity her." Shaking his head, he went through.

Loki stepped out of the gateway and into the backyard of the Nordins, striding past the familiar pole barn and toward the rear door. He moved silently, so no one poked their head out a window to engage him as he crossed the lawn. When he knocked on the door, Jacob, the eldest of Bailey's three younger brothers, answered.

"Oh, hi," the young man said. "We were relaxing after lunch and the funeral service for the guys who died in the elf world. The rest of them are off paying their respects to the families. You need to talk to Bailey?"

He managed a small frown of sympathy. "Indeed I do. Rather important, though not to the point of absolute urgency."

Jacob admitted the mischief-god, and they found Bailey on the couch in the living room, her arm around Roland as the couple and the other two brothers watched TV.

The girl waved. "Hello. Bad news, I'm guessing? I was trying to relax after all the shit we went through earlier. We had to bury one of Will's friends, plus the others. Though of course, I expected you back sooner rather than later."

Loki sat down next to Roland, pressing against him. The wizard made a sour face.

"Yes," the deity replied, "I'm afraid so. Well, mostly bad, but good in the sense that we have absolute, indisputable proof of what we'd suspected, and can therefore act without hesitation."

The girl's face fell, and there was a twinge of pain in the expression. She'd been holding out hope, he suspected, that Fenris was not truly her enemy after all.

But what was going on was far bigger and more important than the emotional security of one young goddess. He could not spare her the truth. As she watched, he extended his hand, summoning the point of light he'd held while recording the battle between Fenris and Balder. With a snap of his fingers, he replayed the entire scene.

Bailey watched with mounting sick horror. She had good control of herself, but it was obvious that it was taking a great deal of effort. In particular, she seemed hurt and disturbed by the cold, flat tone Fenris used when admitting his role in the recent chaos and to his intentions to bring about the end of the world, regardless of who he had to sacrifice.

The other thing that clearly bothered her was the revelation that Carl was working with Fenris and had been in on his plans the whole time. Loki recalled that Bailey and the scion had become friends during their time together at the training grounds.

The girl's mouth fell open. "My God," she gasped. "Loki, I know this is a stupid question, but...are you sure this is real? This is *exactly* what they said and did?"

He let the wry amusement drain out of his face; sometimes, it was better to be serious. "Quite sure," he declared. "I had to be there to observe them in order to record it, and this was what I saw and heard. I don't deceive people when it comes to truly important matters."

After a short pause, he added, "Balder is fine, however. We successfully pulled off the ploy to trick Fenris into *thinking* he'd murdered him."

Dead, absolute silence held sway in the room for about ten seconds. Then Bailey abruptly jumped up and stormed out to the backyard.

Jacob commented, "Let her go. She needs a minute alone. You can talk again when she's ready."

Loki folded his hand, canceling the illusion in the same motion. "So be it. I take it she's accepted what she's seen."

Frowning, Roland remarked, "I think she accepted it a while ago, but in the back of her mind, she didn't want it to be true and was holding out a tiny speck of hope. I suppose it's better for her to be one hundred percent certain today than still be inwardly confused at the very end. There was no avoiding it forever."

Kurt's mouth hung open, and he stared at something far away, or at something within his own head. "Fenris," he stammered, "is...is...he's *our god*. He's the Father of Weres. How could he do this to us? To everyone? I didn't believe it at first, either."

Russell flexed his huge hands and his eyes burned. "There aren't any words for this," he growled.

Jacob only sat holding his downturned face in his hand and sighed. "No one could've anticipated this crap. It doesn't make sense. We'll have to tell all the other Weres that there's no denying or pretending anymore."

Loki agreed, then he wandered through the house toward the rear door before following Bailey to the back-yard. She stood at the edge of her family's property, back to him, looking into the mountains and the sky.

He came to within five feet and waited. "I'm sorry, Bailey."

"Yeah," she responded, her voice low and soft. "Me too."

The god of mischief ran two fingers through his black hair. "He is my son, as well as your people's father, but he's too far gone for us to do anything but stop him. You may take the remainder of the day and the night to rest."

She turned around, and her eyes were red and shiny. Her fists trembled with anger, though her face was mourn-ful. "Then what?"

"In the morning, we depart for Asgard."

CHAPTER NINE

Bailey awoke at 8:22 and decided it was good enough. She'd slept for over seven hours, yet it was still early enough for her to make the necessary preparations for her coming excursion.

As she walked downstairs, sniffing the air for any signs of fresh coffee, she saw at once that preparations must not have been part of the plan. Loki was sitting in a chair in the living room, waiting for her.

"Good morning," he opened. "I hope you rested well. I heard you snoring loudly, which usually seems to mean that it was a good sleep, yes?"

"Uhh," she muttered, her brain not yet operating at full capacity, "yeah, usually. Something like that. Did anyone make coffee?"

Russell poked his massive head out through the dining room doorway. "Yeah," he replied. "It's strong."

Bailey nodded and accepted a cup gratefully. She felt as though she'd been drinking heavily last night, though all she'd had was one beer.

It's got to be the aftereffects of absorbing the dark elven king's power, she surmised. *But it was different in the past. Then again, I was siphoning it from gods. Gormyr was a supernatural creature, but not a frickin' deity. That must be it.*

She sat down in the living room to sip her brother's borderline-dangerous brew, blinking and stretching her limbs one by one.

Loki spoke up. "How do you feel? The sooner we visit Asgard, the better."

She grunted. "Eh. Okay, I guess, but I'm gonna need time for coffee, hopefully breakfast, and a shower. So, like, an hour?"

"Hmm." The god of mischief stroked his smooth chin. "Aim for forty-five minutes."

Fifty minutes later, the werewitch was ready to go. She'd dressed in nice slacks and a blouse. Somehow, she felt like she should be presentable while visiting the home-world of the Norse gods.

Roland wandered in. He'd slept out in the pole barn to create fewer disturbances while his fiancée rested and recovered from the recent battle. He pursed his lips appreciatively at the sight of her.

"Nice! Are you going for a job interview at the bank or something?"

Her head whipped toward him. "No, dork. Like we said yesterday, I'm going to Asgard. Maybe I'm overdressed since I was still wearing the usual blue jeans when we went before the council, but I dunno, this seems different."

Loki came up. "It doesn't matter much, but there's no downside to looking good, is there? Anyway, come. I can't say how long we'll be gone, but one of us will try to send word to your family and friends if it's terribly long."

Jacob had wandered in. He and Roland gave solemn nods and hugged the girl goodbye.

"Don't worry," she told them. "Nothing's killed me yet, and I don't intend to break that streak."

She and the lord of mischief strode out the back door to open a portal behind the pole barn by the pine-forested slopes.

Before they went through, Loki held up a finger in a schoolmarm-like gesture of admonishment.

"Do not let your guard down," he warned Bailey. "Under normal conditions, Asgard is not dangerous to anyone who has business there. As a goddess, you *do*. However, things lately have not been normal conditions. The attacks on the realm's boundaries have everyone on edge, and of course, we are not yet certain if Fenris might have turned anyone to his cause, or who his agents might be if so."

The girl grimaced and nodded. "Got it. Makes sense."

"Another thing," Loki added. "The people of Asgard respect strength. It is a domain where tremendous power, divine, arcane, or physical, is the norm, so don't hide your power. Don't be ashamed of your status as a rising deity. *Flaunt* it. Not in an obnoxious or conceited way, but with calm confidence and quiet grace. Such a bearing will serve you well there, and in other places, too, if need be."

She understood and said so. It didn't sound too different from when she'd had to present herself as a leader before large numbers of Weres and witches.

Loki swept his hand toward the portal with an elaborate, almost swishy gesture. "Very well. After you, my dear."

She stepped through, ignoring the typical brief instant of dizzying cold, and her foot came down on the marble pavement that lined the streets of the city of the gods.

"Wow," she murmured. Loki came out behind her, closed the portal, and allowed her a couple of seconds to take in the sights.

All around them was an airy blue void filled with fast-moving white clouds and bright light that refracted into rainbows against the gleaming surfaces. The city had been built upon the broad, mostly flat top of a mountain, and beyond the main metropolitan area was an island that floated in the sky at a higher level than the rest of the city. There lay the palace of the gods.

Loki took her by the shoulder and led her down the broad avenues as tall, handsome people in strange bright clothes looked her over. Since she was with Loki, they paid little heed to her beyond the first glance.

"In truth," the trickster-god began, "you should have been introduced here sooner. You have every right to a place here, after all."

She glanced around as they walked. In addition to the white marble pavement, there were buildings, domes, and spires of gold and silver, the style sometimes reminiscent of Viking longhouses or tall and narrow Norwegian stave churches, sometimes structures that had no earthly equivalents. The aesthetic was Old Norse, but ten times more grand and glamorous.

She turned her head to Loki. "Question. The council chamber…is that located here? In Asgard, I mean. I was only ever in the main chamber or the hallway leading up to it, so I never saw much of where it was if that makes sense."

Loki nodded. "It lies in Asgard, though distant from this point, near the far upper edge of the domain, where Asgard starts to blend in with other of the 'higher' realms. The city is located at the approximate center. The borders of the realms of the monstrous peoples lie at the lower edges, near the base of the great mountain."

That makes sense, she thought. *Mostly. The stuff about "edges" is weird, but not everyplace works the same way as Earth.*

The broad marble avenues soon led them to a stone arch with warrior statues on either side. The arch lay at the edge of the mountaintop, and below was nothing but a sea of clouds, denser than the ones higher in the sky.

A causeway led to the floating palace, made of what looked like pure, condensed, multicolored light. Bailey stared at it in wonder.

"Bifröst," Loki announced, "the Rainbow Bridge. It will more than support our weight, don't worry." He stepped onto the curved mass of light.

Bailey did likewise. Though she'd flown magically through the air, it was strangely uncomfortable to walk on a translucent surface, looking down between her feet to see nothing whatsoever beneath her. But the bridge held, and its surface seemed "magnetic" in that it exerted a mild pull on her feet with each step, likely to ensure no one fell off.

Halfway across the span, four guardsmen emerged from the gate to the floating palace complex to greet them.

"Hail, Loki," their apparent leader opened. "All is well and secure. If we might ask, is this Bailey Nordin with you?" He looked at the girl with an open, neutral expression.

"Yes," said the black-haired man.

Bailey waved. "Hi. I'm standing in for Freya, at least for the time being. But I'm guessing you heard that."

The man bowed briefly, then he and the others turned to escort them through the gates. They wore armor that looked like it was made of stainless steel and polished gold, though she imagined it was a stronger, divine material. They carried partizan spears and short Viking-style swords at their sides, and sky-blue cloaks trailed behind them in the cool breeze.

Once they passed through the gates, Bailey realized that the central structure upon the floating island was more of a walled complex than a single building, much like the castle at the training grounds, though again, the architecture here was a fantasy or science-fiction extrapolation of traditional Scandinavian styles.

Loki waved a hand to the guardsmen to indicate that the two deities would be fine on their own; they nodded and returned to their posts. Then the trickster god took Bailey into a shadowed corner off one of the main avenues, behind an outbuilding of white stone.

He flicked his hand, and a shimmering curtain surrounded them. "There," he quipped. "We'll look like common attendants to any but the most prying eyes, and no one will be able to hear us speak."

"Okay," she replied. "So, uh, is Odin still in charge? I know he's traditionally the king of Asgard, but you guys have barely mentioned him."

Loki smiled. "I was getting to that. You're quite inquisitive, aren't you? But yes, Odin reigns, and yet does not reign *at the moment*. Therein lies the problem."

Feet tramped by, and Bailey glanced toward them. It was only a pair of soldiers followed by four servants carrying two barrels, perhaps of mead, between them. She relaxed. Scenes from the awful hologram of Fenris killing Balder, or so he thought, while Carl looked on and sneered, kept flashing in her mind, and robbing her of her ability to trust her surroundings.

Loki went on. "The All-Father, at this point in time, rests in the Odin-Sleep. Frigga, his wife, watches over him. They are not present. Thor is the designated heir, but he is not yet ready to assume sovereignty over our realms, so Asgard has no sitting ruler. The throne room within the palace lies empty, and it is there that Fenris likely waits even now."

The girl squinted in confusion. "No one's there to stop him? And nobody thinks it's suspicious that he's prowling around in Odin's place?"

The god of mischief shrugged. "The one who sits on the throne is the important thing. Otherwise, it is merely a chair within a room. The place is ignored when not occupied by its king. Besides, everyone is distracted by the frequent attacks on our borders, which of course, Fenris himself organized."

Loki's face fell and his eyes darkened. "But there is one other purpose that the throne room is capable of serving. It can act as a *ritual chamber*, and Fenris is likely preparing his little ceremony there, but it's not the time to interrupt him. Soon, but not today. We are here on other business. Follow me. What we seek lies within that courtyard over yonder."

He led her down the shining avenue, around a corner, and through a smaller stone arch into a square with a great tree and a fountain at its center. Otherwise, it was carpeted with emerald grass, and friezes depicting scenes from heroic battles adorned the walls.

She estimated it spanned about six acres. It seemed enormous and made her wonder how big the rest of the palace was.

However, she wasn't sure what Loki wanted her to see.

The answer came without delay. Her companion raised his slender hands and announced something in what she supposed was Old Norse or a secret language of the gods, yet it registered in her brain as "Knights of the Grand Legion of Asgard, assemble!"

At once, the courtyard was flooded with an over-whelming cascade of white light, which scattered into streams of rainbow as it struck glass, stone, wood, or the water of the central fountain. As a handy side effect of her newfound divinity, Bailey could mostly look at it, but she still turned her head half away and squeezed her eyes partially shut.

When the light cleared, the courtyard was brimming with armored warriors, lined up and ready for battle.

Loki turned to the girl. "I am placing them under your command. We have an incursion to deal with; the frost trolls are once again plaguing the lower slopes of our mountain. Their leader, King Imrit, has assembled a vast host, possibly strong enough to breach our defenses."

Gawking, the girl nodded and stared at her new army.

The men were almost identical to one another, and they resembled Balder, she thought, though they were somewhat less radiantly beautiful, and red or golden beards adorned their chins. Their armor was much like that of the guards on Bifröst, shining steel and silver, and they all carried long lances, partizans, or halberds, as well as short swords and round, gold-rimmed shields. The capes they wore were crimson rather than blue. She guessed this was to indicate that they were a military rather than a police force.

Loki addressed the soldiers. "Bailey Nordin is the newly-ascended goddess of sorcery and werewolves. She sits upon the seat which formerly belonged to Lady Freya, warming it as its steward, as we of the council agreed to. Obey Bailey as you would obey Freya. Follow her lead and trust her judgment, for she has commanded successful expeditions before. Furthermore, as a pupil of Fenris the Wolf-Father, she is well-versed in magic and esoterica. Thus she has the blessings of the full pantheon."

Before Bailey could ask about that, Loki added to her in a low voice, "What you learned last night is not yet public knowledge, nor does it need to be—yet. The time will come soon."

So, she surmised, *the general populace here doesn't know the truth about Fenris yet. That's probably another reason why no one stopped him from going into the throne room.*

"They will follow you," Loki continued, "even unto the final battle, when, or should we say *if*, that comes to pass. Do not fear to use their courage and strength, but hold their lives as valuable all the same, like you have in the past with your own people."

The werewitch put her hands on her hips. "I understand. Will do."

The god of mischief went on, addressing both her and the Asgardian Army. "The frost trolls have made our existence more difficult with their ill-planned harrying strikes, and it seems that now they've amassed a gigantic host for a full assault upon the realm's borders, seeking to break through and overrun our capital. The hour in which we stop them once and for all is nigh."

Bailey told the troops, "I've fought the frost trolls before. It was just Fenris and me, and we made short work of the bastards. With all you men at my side, I'm sure we can handle them. I'll give you general instructions, but I'll otherwise assume you can fight without being micromanaged. I will provide the heaviest offense to soften them up at the start."

Loki touched her shoulder and whispered in her ear. "We must repel this attack, of course, but by sending you against the trolls, Fenris will continue to assume that you're not aware of his plot. Go! And good luck."

"Noted. And thanks."

It occurred to her that she felt somehow faster and that her understanding of magic had deepened. The power she'd drawn from King Gormyr must have settled within her.

Loki opened a portal wide enough for five men abreast and motioned for Bailey to go through first. Sucking in her breath, she did, and the soldiers of Asgard marched through behind her.

The locale into which they emerged looked familiar; it was the same broad snowy plain narrowing behind her as it ascended into a mountain pass where she and Fenris had teleported before. Up ahead lay the dense forest where the frost trolls had gathered before their prior attacks. Fat snowflakes drifted down from the clear sky.

This time, the enemy army was assembled. Half the plain was covered by a dense mass of hulking humanoid bodies, grunting and waving their clubs and crude swords and axes in the air. Bailey and the divine army had caught the trolls mere moments before they'd launch their invasion.

Their numbers were far greater than what she and Fenris had faced previously, thousands rather than hundreds. The rear echelons stretched beyond the plain and into the woods. For all she knew, the entire forest might have been packed, every available space between the trees filled with trolls.

She raised her arm and bellowed, "Get ready!" She herself wasted no time.

Bailey pointed at the horde, which had perked up and started to howl upon noticing her and the Asgardians. A nuclear explosion went off, front and center of the host. Bailey immediately conjured a powerful shield in front of her, keeping the effects of the blast from harming her allies.

The destruction it wrought on the trolls was terrifying. A high dome, virtually a column, of blazing light ascended into the sky, along with a roar that shook the earth. Smoke and debris spread out to the sides. An entire third of the troll army, or at least the portion visible on the treeless plain, had been vaporized, leaving only blackened earth behind. Snow by the edges of the blast radius melted and turned the scorched ground to mud.

Bailey produced her sword. She did not fully understand how, but she had bonded to the weapon in such a way that it came to her whenever she commanded it to, regardless of where it had last been left. She raised it over her head.

"Charge!" she screamed.

She and the trolls did exactly as she'd said, barreling toward one another at top speed. When she looked back over her shoulder, she saw the Asgardian troops advancing, though at a trot rather than a sprint. Furthermore, instead of plunging straight ahead, they moved sidelong toward an elevated position where boulders and the foothills of the nearby mountain covered part of their right flank and rear. Then they assumed a phalanx formation.

Good for them, Bailey thought. *They're the smart type of warriors. Isn't that a Greek formation, though? Whatever. I probably should have hung back and waited for them.*

But there was no time to change her mind.

She crashed into the first dozen trolls, blowing half of them into the air with a burst of sonic, kinetic, and electrical force that broke most of their bones and liquefied their brains. Then she darted about, zig-zagging between them, jumping over their heads or ducking under their weapons while she slashed.

Her movements were frenzied yet controlled. The enchanted blade cleaved through limbs and organs, and she conjured enough shield matter around her to deflect most of the force of their powerful blows, knocking them off-balance if they struck the arcane barriers. Then they became easy prey.

As trolls died around the girl, she spared a quick look at her allies. They'd drawn off half or more of the monstrous host and were fighting defensively against the undisciplined charge of the creatures. Their long polearms stabbed knees and hearts, felling the majority of the trolls before they could get in range to smash at the Asgardians with their brutish weaponry.

Bailey dashed to the side, seeking to fight her way back to the troops. It was better for them not to be divided. She blasted a cluster of trolls away from her, then concentrated and threw her sword laterally so it spun like a buzzsaw through the monsters' ranks, killing twenty of them before burying itself in the snow near the phalanx.

She shifted into wolf form, allowing herself to swell to full size so she was as big as the trolls. She could magically reconstitute her dress clothes later. In the heat of battle, she had more pressing things to worry about.

Bounding at the full speed of a beast of the woods, she tore through the already-shaky lines of her foes, shouldering some aside, slashing them with her claws or ripping out throats or hamstrings as needed. Axes and clubs struck at her from the sides, but her shields were still up, and the mightiest of their blows only knocked her slightly off-course.

Seconds later, she stood before her sword. The girl shifted back to human form and retrieved it, conjuring a decent replica of her former outfit as she drew it from the snow.

One of the soldiers, probably an officer, stepped forth. "Lady Bailey, are you all right? What orders next? They'll be upon us again in a heart's beat."

It was true. Though they'd devastated huge numbers of

the beasts, thousands remained, and they were closing in, snarling and furious.

"I'm fine," she answered the lieutenant. "We'll hold off the next charge, then we need to go on the offensive. I'll hit them with everything I have magically and break up their lines. You guys follow me and finish off the stragglers."

The officer nodded. "As you wish."

Another wave of trolls piled toward them, kicking up the mud from the earlier explosion combined with meltwater. Once they reached the deep snow again, Bailey raised all of it in a white rushing cloud, melting it further and driving the beasts back on a torrent of water that thickened with mud as it flowed over the barren patch.

Then she clenched her fist, freezing it all solid. Some trolls were trapped within the ice and died quickly. Others were stuck half-in and were easy prey for the lances of the Asgardian soldiers. The phalanx advanced.

More trolls streamed out of the woods. Aside from the piles of scattered bodies, it was as though Bailey's force had barely made a dent in their numbers.

She hoisted her sword, using it to channel all manner of destructive spells, and bolted ahead. She tried to keep from outdistancing her men too far but nonetheless worked gradually ahead of them, cleaving and blasting left and right, wreaking havoc and dividing the enemy.

The werewitch didn't stop to kill the wounded or disoriented, leaving that to her troops. Soon, the field was clear of living adversaries. Many still hovered around the edge of the field or regrouped in the shadows of the trees.

Bailey caught her breath, wiping sweat from her face and blood from her sword.

Most of the trolls had withdrawn, but they had not retreated. They were rallying, tightening their formation around a central point beyond the edge of the forest. Bailey cut through two more of the stragglers to get closer, then jumped into the air and floated fifty feet above the battle to see what was going on.

The frost trolls' king, Imrit, had taken the field, emerging from the trees. He was the biggest of them all, and his presence had instilled renewed confidence in his warriors. Not to mention he was giving them orders, forcing them to obey simple tactics instead of fighting as a mass of individual berserkers.

Worse still, trolls from the rear guard were pushing forward contraptions that Bailey recognized as catapults. They were so crudely-built that she'd almost mistaken them for totemic idols, but they had counterweighted arms and were loaded with odd bluish projectiles.

She flew back toward the ground and also closer to the troll army. The things in the catapults were huge chunks of ice that blazed and shimmered with unknown magic.

"Crap!" she growled, plunging to the ground and cutting a half-dozen trolls down with a blade-thin wave of concentrated plasma.

The king bellowed something and the siege engines fired. Bailey shot down two of the frosty boulders with bolts of fire, but one landed near the front of the Asgardian phalanx. It struck the ground, kicking up snow and releasing a blue shockwave that flash-froze at least twenty soldiers. Their bodies turned into statues of ice, fell over, and broke apart.

The girl gritted her teeth. "No, goddammit!" They'd lost

only a small fraction of the hundreds of soldiers who'd come with her, but she refused to lose any more.

She turned and glared at King Imrit.

I'm supposed to kill him and take his power, right? she reflected. *Pretty sure that's what I'd do regardless. Get ready, you son of a bitch.*

CHAPTER TEN

Bailey hurled herself into the center of the maelstrom. The sky was blotted out by the tall, thick bodies and hairy limbs of the trolls, and the air was filled with the powerful swipes of their weapons. She battered aside all comers, or split the creatures asunder with her sword, or blasted them to pieces.

Each time she heard the thunking sound of the catapults being fired, she immediately created an inverted rainstorm of plasma, thousands of blazing projectiles streaking into the sky to destroy the ice-bombs before they could reach her soldiers.

Moments later, the lines of the dying trolls parted and their titanic monarch stood before her, hefting a gargantuan club made from an entire tree trunk which was spiked with magically-augmented icicles.

"Imrit!" she cried, "King of the frost trolls! I am Bailey Nordin, called Nova, and I challenge you to single combat. Cease all fighting and let the battle be decided by us alone. Winner takes all!"

He stared at her with beady eyes full of primitive anger and dull arrogance. He barked something to his warriors, presumably telling them to stand down since they stopped where they stood and parted to form a broad circle.

"*Yes,*" Imrit growled, "we will fight, Bailey Nordin. No magic or deal is off. You will die without magic, and then Asgard falls!"

She said nothing, only stood with her sword aimed at his face, nodding her agreement to his conditions.

Roaring like an enraged bear, Imrit flew at her, wielding his great club with a speed and ferocity that belied his ungainly appearance.

Her first instinct was to shield herself, ignoring the deal they'd made, but that would be both dishonorable and stupid. She'd end up having to fight all his warriors as well, and they'd resume their bombardment of the Asgardians.

Instead, she relied on the enhanced agility she'd siphoned from Gormyr, added to the superhuman speed and strength she already possessed as both goddess and werewitch.

Fast though he was, Imrit lacked subtlety and telegraphed his moves with brief yet obvious wind-ups. Speed and pure force were on his side, but he hadn't heard of feinting.

Bailey hopped over his swings or rolled under them, prepared to dash to one side and then darted to another. Imrit resumed his berserk whirlwind of wrath. The ground vibrated under the stomping of his feet and the impacts of his swings. He struck with greater intensity, but not with greater intelligence.

I can outlast him, the girl concluded, *but without a magic shield, one hit and I'm done. It'll be tough to hit him without leaving myself open.*

Against such a huge opponent, whose offensive reach was nearly triple her own, her longsword didn't seem particularly long. She tried rolling between Imrit's legs as he prepared an overhead strike and extended the blade upward as part of the motion, cutting through the troll king's thigh.

He howled in pain and whirled to face her as she regained her feet and backed away. Drool ran around his tusks. He raised his off-hand and the air shimmered with a deep-blue glowing mist that coalesced in his grip as a double-headed battle-axe made of the same ensorcelled ice as the catapults' payloads.

"Hey!" Bailey protested. "That's magic!"

"Only weapon!" he barked. "Now fight!"

Frowning, she raised her sword and surrounded it with heat so that the blade burst into golden flames. "Only fair," she pronounced.

Imrit was too intent on killing her to renegotiate the deal. He plunged ahead, spinning as he moved, both his giant weapons filling the air with the potential for violent death.

At first, Bailey reacted as she had before, concentrating on dodging the monarch and hoping to tire him out, but his strength didn't seem to flag. She opted to try a gamble; it was risky, but...

She extended her sword in such a way that Imrit's axe would strike it straight on at a ninety-degree angle. The blue blade streaked through the air.

Then it shattered into a mass of glowing ice chunks against the flaming blade of Bailey's divine sword.

"What?" Imrit raged. "No! *No!*"

Bailey seized the initiative by leaping over his club-arm, landing on his shoulder, and stabbing down into the place where his neck and chest met. He raised a hand to crush her and fling her off, but she jumped away, slashing him down the back as she descended.

Imrit again attacked, furious but slowing. Spots of his blood appeared on the snow.

The werewitch evaded him. Now his attacks *were* flagging. She'd be able to deliver the *coup de grace* as soon as he made a mistake.

Imrit lost sight of her briefly as she ducked under an overextended swing on his part. It was the last error he ever made.

Bailey shot upward behind him, raising her sword like an icepick and plunging it into the back of the troll king's neck. His cry turned into a gurgle, and he fell to his knees. As his life seeped out, the girl, knowing she'd won, sent out her tendrils, locking them into his aura to drain his power.

The well of it was deeper than she'd expected. For all their primitive stupidity, the frost trolls were ancient beings with well-developed lore, tremendous endurance, and magical protection from the elements of snow and ice, along with a limited ability to manipulate those same elements. The rush of strength and wisdom was nearly paralyzing.

Imrit fell face-down in the snow and moved no more. Bailey withdrew her sword and stood facing the circle of his fighters.

"Okay," she ground out, "as per the deal I made with your king, I won, so that means—"

"*Kill her!*" one of them choked.

The girl's face fell. "Shit."

A virtual avalanche of trolls and troll-clubs and troll-axes descended on her. The werewitch launched herself straight up into the sky, evading their blows by a heartbeat, then flying over them to regroup with the soldiers of Asgard.

The troops rushed to meet her as the horde spun and made ready to begin the pitched battle anew.

"Okay," Bailey told the warriors, "that didn't work. Looks like we have to kill 'em all."

The catapults fired. Bailey turned, instantly conjuring a shield and adding to it part of the new magic she'd absorbed from Imrit. The translucent barrier took on a distinctive blue tint.

The enchanted ice boulders ricocheted cleanly off the shield with extra force, relative to the velocity they'd come in at. The effect was like two magnets of the same charge repelling one another. The projectiles landed amidst the trolls and exploded. They had a natural resistance to cold magic, so they did not flash-freeze or die, but the burst still seemed to cause them pain and slow their movements.

"Hah!" Bailey hefted her sword. "All right, let's try this again. *Charge!*"

Fenris watched as the Asgardian legion, with the werewitch at its head, finished off the last of King Imrit's mighty horde. Carl stood a pace or two behind him and to the side, peering over his shoulder into the mirror-like disc that disclosed the scene to them.

The scion whistled. "My, my. Quite the slaughter, isn't it?"

"Yes," Fenris stated, his voice low and monotone. "She has grown stronger, and destroyed most of the trolls who were willing and able to fight. Of course, some of their species still remain: women, children, the elderly, and small splinter tribes beyond Imrit's authority. But it will be another generation, perhaps two or three before they can attempt anything on this level again. Not that it matters. They have served their purpose."

He waved his hand, and the crystal disc went dark. It was one of two mounted on wooden stands in the throne room, the Eye of Huginn to the right of Odin's seat. The Eye of Muninn sat to the left.

The wolf-father turned back to the business in which he and his apprentice had been engrossed before they'd checked on the girl.

The throne room was both grand and austere. Its walls were of smooth gray stone hung with blue and red tapestries depicting knots, ships, warriors, and wolves. The chamber had no furniture nor decoration save the mirrors, the dais of the throne, a pair of golden braziers, and the throne itself. The chair was of oak, tall but spartan, with only a blue cushion to adorn it. There were no windows. The air of the place was somber and contemplative, like Odin the All-Father.

The floor differed from the walls and ceiling in being matte black marble. All across it, Fenris and Carl had drawn a sequence of signs and sigils in the traditional red-ochre ink used for rituals of high ceremonial magic. The last couple of runes still needed to be completed.

Fenris dipped a slant-cut reed into the hollow sheep skull in which he'd stored the dye. As he returned to work, he spoke.

"Bailey should be ready. If not entirely, then so close as to make little difference. We ought to put her through at least one more battle. There are two more armies of monsters massing. That should bring her up to exactly the level of my power. And, of course, it will keep her busy while we enact the final steps."

He touched the reed-quill to the floor and traced a curious design, linking it to one he'd drawn a short while before. When the sequence was complete, they would be ready to cast the spell at the veritable heart of the Norse divine realm and the Asgardian empire, which would bring about the Beginning of the End and the Twilight of the Gods.

Only the sacrifice would remain to be performed.

"Hmm," Carl opined. "Yes, probably a good idea, my lord. We don't want her *too* powerful though, do we? And she jumped the proverbial gun on the frost trolls. Will we have time to complete our preparations before she takes on the rock giants or the draugar?"

Fenris grunted. "I had planned to set her against Imrit as soon as we were finished with the runes, anyway. It makes no difference that she came to that conclusion on her own, or possibly at the council's urging."

"Speaking of which," Carl interjected, "aren't there a

few more 'targets' for us to eliminate? Balder was only the beginning, wasn't he?"

The hooded man nodded. "We should go after Thoth next. As the god of wisdom, he may be among those smart enough to grasp what is happening and attempt to interfere before we're done. Leaving him alive too long could create unnecessary hassles."

"Agreed." Carl beamed, pleased with himself in advance. Clearly he had something to share. "In fact, because I agree, it shouldn't shock you to learn that I've been tracking the old Egyptian prick on and off, and I just checked up on him recently."

"Oh?" Fenris inquired without looking up from his rune-work.

The scion went on. "Yes. He's having a nice leisurely stroll through a nasty desert stretch of the Other, a place that reminds him of the sandy wastes on either side of the Nile, I suppose. It seems he was weary of his duties and wanted to recharge before the shit hit the fan here in Asgard, so he retreated to that godforsaken spot seeking clarity, reflection, peace, and that sort of thing. In *isolation*, naturally."

Now Fenris did look up, and he smiled. "How nice of him to be alone and far from help," he commented. "Help me finish this final sigil, then we will ambush him together."

"Certainly." Carl knelt, taking up a spare reed and smoothing the edges of Fenris' bold lines. The runes were completed in minutes.

They both stood. They had no fear of interruption or discovery since they'd surrounded the throne room with multiple spells: one to discourage the will of any who might peek in, another to create an illusion of the chamber being empty and normal, and a third to physically repel anyone who tried to step in regardless. If *that* raised suspicions, most Asgardians would assume they were put there by Odin.

None of them had any idea about what was coming.

Fenris concentrated on Thoth's energy signature as Carl helped him narrow it down by describing the section of the Other in more detail. It lay near the red-rock canyon realm where the witch-specters had recently aggregated, far from the swamps that formed the main central region. Fenris knew of the place but had little experience with it.

"Ah," the wolf-god murmured, "I've found him. Let us pay him a visit."

He raised his hands, chanted, and opened a purple gateway in the air before Odin's throne. They stepped through and closed it behind them.

Moving from the mild climate of Asgard to the brief cold of astral travel, the two then emerged under a blazing hot sun. The sky, a flat, nondescript metallic color, was clear of clouds. The landscape around them was featureless save for endless dunes of pale brown sand.

There was no sign of the lord of wisdom. Fenris touched the side of his head and looked toward a line of dunes tall enough to be mistaken for low mountains. "He is beyond those. Come."

They trudged through the erg, making little effort to conceal themselves. Thoth had not bothered to hide his aura since the region was uninhabited, and he would have had no reason to suppose anyone was hunting him. If anything, he wanted to keep himself easy to find in case he was needed back in Asgard. And he was stationary, probably meditating.

Fenris crested the tall dunes first, with Carl close behind. They looked down into a curiously shaped narrow little valley between two serpentine ridges of sand. Thoth sat at the bottom, cross-legged, his eyes shut. Beside him was a tiny pool of water beside which a single date palm tree and a handful of green fronds grew.

Without opening his eyes or turning his head, Thoth greeted them in his deep voice. "Hello, Fenris the Wolf-Father. Hello, Carl the Scion. I am not surprised you've found me."

"Oh?" said Fenris. "It was not difficult." He took two slow, heavy steps down the slope, dislodging a small, hissing flow of sand.

The Egyptian deity did open his eyelids then and slowly rose to his feet to look up at his visitors. "I was quite aware you were up to something. The precise nature of it, no, but you would be a fool to assume that your recent irregularities of behavior were lost on me. Perhaps you *are* a fool at that. You're certainly not as smart as you like to think."

Fenris stopped, frowned, and then advanced again. "And you," he stated, "are, as the humans say, too smart for your own good. Your supercilious and pretentious attitude has always made a fine counterpoint to the ignorance and naïveté of Balder. The *late* Balder."

Carl had begun to circle toward Thoth's flank. "Since you're so wise, O Great God of Wisdom," quipped the scion, "you were aware that Balder was dead, right?"

Thoth didn't answer. His dark, aged face only grimaced.

His eyes were clear and open, not bothered by the bright sun.

Fenris stopped at the base of the tall dune. "It will be good to be rid of you. Balder was wounded and weak, so he did not give me as much sport as I would have liked. But you, old one, are at full strength, or as close to full as can be expected at your age."

"At my age," Thoth retorted, "I have seen the rise and fall of greater beings than—"

Fenris struck him full in the chest with a sudden bolt of lightning, while Carl sprang in and kicked the wisdom-god's legs out from under him. But before he struck the ground, he was gone. In his place, a hissing swarm of poisonous asps moved through the dust.

Carl sprang back, searing the sand beneath him with a gout of blue-white flame that turned it to glass. Two of the snakes were destroyed, but the rest had separated and made toward Fenris.

The wolf-god leaped into the air, hurling bolts of concentrated percussive force into the base of the great dune, collapsing it in an avalanche of sand that buried the serpents. By the time he landed on the earth next to the small oasis, Thoth had sprung free of the particulate mass, back in human form, his eyes glowing white with wrath.

At a motion of his hand, the water in the tiny pool surged upward in a gout far larger and more powerful than anything the oasis could have mustered under natural conditions and formed into an ibis-like construct of foaming liquid. The bird dive-bombed Fenris, its body separating into a storm of icy knives.

The wolf-god was in motion, springing past the impact

point of the icicles and shifting into his huge wolf-form. He tackled Thoth in a flurry of sand, and the two figures wrestled while Carl moved in to harry the Egyptian with plasma lances, tripwires of condensed atmospheric metals, and psionic waves of confusion.

Thoth faltered, but he summoned all his strength and threw Fenris off of him, causing the massive wolf to roll to the bottom of the valley.

Before the lord of wisdom could counterattack, Fenris struck him from three sides simultaneously with lightning, briefly paralyzing him. Carl moved in from the fourth side and punched him in the jaw after surrounding his fist with an arcane shield. Thoth's head snapped back, and he collapsed in the dust.

He regained his feet quickly enough, but the interplay of the two combatants—a god who was his equal and a demigod only marginally weaker than himself—wore him down. Soon Thoth could barely defend himself.

Fenris roared in vicious triumph and seized the aged dark-skinned deity in his jaws, whipping him back and forth, then hurling him to the ground and stomping on him with his clawed forelegs, while Carl continuously blasted him with arcane and elemental attacks.

Thoth tried to get back up, only to stumble to his knees. "Uhh," he gasped. "So be it. You have won, Fenris, but do not celebrate your victory too soon." He coughed, spitting up ambrosiac ether, and his hands trembled as he clutched his wounds.

Fenris slashed his throat with the claws of his left paw. Then he shifted back into his humanoid form to watch Thoth die.

The Egyptian god faded like a desert mirage, and a snaky mixture of spiraling strands in amber, white, and deep turquoise erupted from his form. What little remained of him dissolved into dust and was lost amidst the desert sand.

Carl let out a gasping sigh. "Woah! Finally. That was harder than dealing with Balder, wasn't it?"

"Yes," Fenris acknowledged, "but not by much. And now another of the oh-so-mighty council has fallen."

Loki watched, slowly shaking his head, though his hands were clenched in the necessary gestures to maintain the illusion, keeping it as convincing as possible right up until the bitter end. At the same time, he was recording the proceedings, as he had during the Balder incident. It put a certain amount of strain on him, but he managed.

"Fenris, Fenris." He sighed. "Where and when, exactly, did you go so wrong?"

The were-god and his apprentice departed through a portal without bothering to absorb the dissipated energy. Again.

Loki finished creating the hologram, processing it as a memory, and once more sending it to the other deities for immediate mental viewing. He stored the visual version within himself for display to Bailey and the mortals later.

"Showing them this might be redundant," the mischief-lord mused, "but it eliminates every last iota of doubt. My son is beyond all hope of salvage or redemption, it would seem."

He did not feel much emotion about that since the sentiments that mortals treasured registered with him only in a vague, intellectual way. Such was his nature. Still, he noticed a deep regret within himself and, more pressingly, a concern—even a fear—for what happened next if Fenris was not stopped.

"Soon," he mumbled to no one, making ready to leave. "I've been saying that too often lately, but it's true. *Soon*."

CHAPTER ELEVEN

Bailey sat in the snow, heedless of the sub-freezing temperatures. The Asgardian troops had made three or four bonfires out of wood debris recovered from the battle, but the werewitch sat apart from them.

She'd needed time to "digest" her new powers, as usual. The strength of the frost trolls' king was different from any arcane source she'd drained before, but it was oddly familiar. There was a primal, animal-like quality to it that reminded her of nothing so much as her own heritage as a lycanthrope. The frost trolls were creatures of snow and icy winds, just as werewolves were creatures of moonlight, fern, and tree-shadow.

The lieutenant she'd spoken to before came over. His name was Sigfred, she recalled.

"Lady Bailey, will we be staying here? The battle is won, and the men would do well to return home." The light was fading; the frost trolls' domain did not have a true day-night cycle, but it seemed to grow dimmer and then brighter in equal turns.

She stood up, wrinkling her brow in thought. "Someone should remain to keep watch, in case more of them try to attack." Five or six hundred had fled toward the end of the battle. "And I'm having trouble adjusting to all the new powers I got. Is there a problem on you guys' end?"

"The cold," Sigfred gasped. "We are hardy, and the exertion of battle warms us, but the frigidity of this realm...we will not be able to fight here indefinitely."

Bailey recalled that in the city and palace of Asgard, the temperature has seemed exceedingly mild despite the sky-high location. She wasn't sure exactly what these men *were* —probably demigods or magical beings similar to the dark elves—but they lacked the arcane ability to completely protect themselves from harsh elements.

"Okay," she said, "well, I think I can do something about that. Hold onto your helmets."

Expanding her consciousness, she created a protective shield-dome around their encampment. It was thinner than a combat shield; a man could push through it with effort, and an arrow or fireball would be slowed rather than stopped, but it would hold in air, allowing the fires to warm it more easily. She poked holes in the barrier near the base and top to allow breathable air to filter in and wood smoke to filter out.

Then she tried another technique. Using part of the newly-absorbed cold-resistance magic, she spread it across the mass of soldiers the way she'd cast a mild healing spell. Blue light played about them as they stared in surprise, then it was gone.

"Better?" she asked. "I'm hoping that will give you more resilience to this place."

Heads nodded, and the men all seemed more comfortable.

The werewitch smiled. "Nice! Admittedly I didn't know if it'd work. Anyway, I need to leave, but I'll be back. What I'm going to suggest is that maybe a quarter or a third of you stay here, and the rest can go back to Asgard. But stay in touch in case you need reinforcements, and be prepared to relieve each other in shifts. That way, everyone can get some rest within the next day or two, but we'll still have a cursory force here to deter any more attacks. Oh, and send word to me if anything major happens."

Sigfred agreed and spoke to the men to divide them into shift groups.

Satisfied, Bailey bade them farewell and opened a doorway leading back to her home.

She stepped out of the portal and into the bronzed light of late afternoon. Her adventure first in Asgard and then in the troll realm had felt like at least a day, but back on Earth, it seemingly had been only half of one, unless she'd been gone for over thirty hours.

Within the house, only Kurt was present in front of the TV. "Hi," he greeted his sister. "Once more, I've been given the illustrious duty of guarding the fucking living room while everyone else goes out and does 'interesting' stuff. Did you have a nice, uh, job interview with the gods?"

She put her hands on her hips but paused to check her clothes. They weren't the same as the ones she'd shredded when she shifted into full-sized wolf form, but close enough.

"I already *have* a job with the gods," she pointed out, "but yeah, things are fine so far. If you see or hear from anyone, tell them I'm back. To be honest, I think I could use a little alone time anyway. I'll be home this evening, though."

After freshening up, Bailey realized she was famished. She wasn't sure if metabolism worked the same way in the supernatural realms as it did here, but the battle against the trolls felt as though it had burned about eight thousand calories.

She hopped into her black Tundra and drove it to the Bristling Elk, annoyed that she was hitting the place right during the dinner rush, but there was no way she was waiting until later to eat.

Tomi noticed her at once. "Oh, hi, Bailey. Are you going for a job interview somewhere?"

"Naw," the girl replied, "all my shitty clothes are dirty."

An old couple sitting in the corner frowned at her language, but Tomi laughed it off.

Half an hour later, Bailey sat before an empty mug of coffee and a mostly-empty plate; she'd ordered an outright steak instead of a steak sandwich, along with extra fries, and a small portion remained. It felt good to have a bellyful of meat.

She looked up from the table at the same moment a fiftyish Native man in blue jeans and a red shirt came in. Unsurprisingly, he made straight for her table.

"Hello, Bailey," he opened.

"Hi, Coyote." She waved to the chair across from her. "Have a seat. I'm sure you planned to anyway."

He lowered himself into place and said, "Indeed. Are you well?"

"Mostly." She went on to briefly summarize all that had happened since they'd last seen each other.

The trickster god gave an appreciative nod. "Well, then. Congratulations on your victories, though we're both aware that the real enemy wanted you to win, as well."

She scowled. "Yeah, I know. But according to Loki, we have to keep playing along. Any updates on that whole situation?"

"Yes." Tomi appeared and asked if Coyote wanted anything. He ordered a root beer, and she hurried off to get it. "In fact," the deity went on, "that's what I came here to talk about. Fenris and Carl have taken out another of us. Thoth, specifically, or so they think."

The waitress returned with the drink, refilled Bailey's coffee, and left them to their discussion as the girl finished off the last of her food.

"Damn," Bailey muttered around a mouthful of steak fries. "He's not wasting time, is he? Usually he's the one who drags me off to fight monsters, so maybe the fact that Loki did it this time spurred him to move quicker or something. Who all does that leave?"

Coyote chuckled. "Me. Probably. I'm the logical next target. But our plan has worked thus far, and there's no reason to believe it won't again. We'll still be watching and offering our protection and guidance from afar. You must keep doing what you're doing, gaining power, neutralizing threats, and preparing for the final confrontation."

She sighed. "Easier said than done, but all right."

The man continued, "Time is growing short, but take a brief respite to acclimate to your new powers. Including this." He reached out and tapped her temple with the first two fingers of his right hand.

She felt as though an echo went through her brain, then everything grew louder. "Uh," she mumbled, "thanks?"

Coyote laughed softly. "A piece of my abilities; you may find it useful. Like Loki, I am a trickster deity, though our approaches are somewhat different. I'm used to the more insidious and convoluted side of magic, so what I've given you is a sort of inner filter that will protect you from the worst aspects of those new strains of knowledge and power bubbling away within you. It will make it easier to process it all."

She blinked. "Well, thanks. That ought to help a lot."

He stood up, having finished his root beer, and laid a five-dollar bill on the table. "Don't mention it. Oh, and another thing that is useful is emotional grounding. Meaning, solace from strife and uncertainty with things, or people who evoke the feelings of peace, love, trust, and comfort. Recharge yourself, then return to the fray."

They waved their goodbyes, and he was gone.

Bailey added the five he'd left to the pool of what she planned to use to pay for her meal, his drink, and the tip, confident of how best to heed his advice.

"Fuckin' hell," Gunney grated, "does this godawful bullshit ever end?" He flipped his cap off his head and blew upward from his mouth to get his shaggy, sweaty hair out of his eyes.

Bailey shrugged. "Doesn't seem like it, but I think it will calm down a lot once we're done with the plan and you-know-who is stopped."

Then again, she'd hoped that before and always been disappointed. Since the fateful day Roland had rolled into town, she was pretty sure that a month had been the longest stretch of peace she'd had. Usually, much less than that.

They both sipped beer. The place was closed for the night, and as the owner of the shop, Gunney had the authority to permit his employees to drink on company grounds.

The mechanic sighed. "Well, maybe my attempt at, y'know, consoling you won't matter much, with the weight of the apocalypse resting on your shoulders, but they say it's the thought that counts."

"It does count," she affirmed, putting her hand on his.

After she'd shown up and they'd hugged and said their hellos, she'd told him about everything that had transpired: Fenris' betrayals and supposed murders of two more gods, the news of Carl's duplicity, the fact that the other deities were enacting their own counter-deception to draw Fenris out, and her two battles against the elves and trolls. Gunney had briefly attended the funeral for Will Waldsbach's friend after the fight against the *alfar*, so that part wasn't news to him.

"All I can say," the old man offered, "is that the events are out of your hands. You didn't do anything to *make* all this happen. Not your fault. Those guys came up with this shit long before you were born and never paused to think about whether it was a good idea, so no need to agonize over how or why it came down the pipeline. But you've got to face it, from the sound of things. Focus on your duty. You've always been good at staring down the beast or whatever and kicking whatever ass you have to. Standing up for what's right, all that corny shit. Corny, but true. Like I've said before, one thing at a time."

She hugged him again. "You have said that before, but sometimes it helps to hear it again."

"I'm sure it sounds stupid," he went on, "and that facing it all will be difficult, but thinking of it that way, it becomes simple."

They stood up, tossing their beer cans into the returns tub.

Bailey said, "I don't much feel up to working on a car."

Shrugging, Gunney suggested, "How about a race, then? You got enough spunk left for it? Besides, we only had one beer each. That's within the legal limit, I think."

She laughed. "Sure. It's dark, though. We haven't raced at night before. You'll be at an unfair disadvantage since I've got were-vision and all that crap."

The mechanic snorted. "Were-vision! No substitute for experience. I was racing cars when you were still an embryo."

Gunney waited at the shop, readying his '65 Shelby Cobra as Bailey drove her Tundra back home, left it there, and returned with her black Camaro. They drove to the edge of town, stopping at the mouth of a long side street that went to the base of the mountain.

The mechanic poked his head out the window. "So, let's

not bother going up the mountain this time. A short sprint to the No Passing sign, that's all. And if you can make us invisible in case Sheriff Browne or one of his boys is lurking up ahead, so much the better."

Bailey agreed to his terms and cast a spell to make them both invisible and soundless. She'd have to reverse it if other motorists appeared, but it wasn't a well-traveled road at night.

They counted down to three and then hit the gas.

To the girl's surprise, Gunney pulled out ahead of her within the first two seconds and stayed there. He cannily anticipated her attempts to pass him and cut her off each time, casually holding her behind as he sped his way to victory. Both drivers blazed past the No Passing post and took their feet off the pedals, slowing to a stop as the road inclined and began to twist around the base of the peak.

The older man climbed out of his beloved car. "Ha, ha," he chortled. "Nice try."

"Damn," Bailey muttered. "Usually either I win, or at least it's, you know, *close*."

Gunney spread his hands. "I've been going easy on you all this time. Tonight, the gloves came off. I might be getting old, but I still have a couple tricks up my sleeve."

She must have looked more disgruntled than she felt since the mechanic came over to lay a hand gently on her shoulder. "Don't feel bad. Anyway, sometimes it's better to let the other person win. Consider that another piece of advice, I guess."

Bailey was about to protest that in the struggle with Fenris she wouldn't have that luxury, but that only emphasized that most things in life weren't anywhere near as important. Thinking about that, she relaxed.

"So," Gunney wrapped up, "back to the shop. I think we need to eliminate another beer. It'll help you sleep, aside from waking up to pee. Just be careful on the drive back home."

Bailey had passed out shortly after midnight and had expected to be out for a good eight hours, a decent and standard "full night's sleep." Instead, when she rolled over and glanced at her clock, it read 12:11. She might have slept later still if she'd been allowed to since it was pounding on her door that roused her.

"Uhh," she groaned. "Yeah, I'm awake. Who are you people, and what do you want with me?"

Jacob's voice asked, "Can we come in?"

"Sure, why not?" She had a sheet over her, and she wore a t-shirt and pajama shorts.

The door opened and Jacob stepped in, with Kurt hovering beside him. "You've got guests, and they want to talk ASAP. We tried to stall them, but you know how it is with people wanting to talk to you. Always something urgent and scary."

She rubbed her eyes. "Who?"

Jacob started to clear his throat, but Kurt spoke first. He put a hand beside his mouth and whispered, *"The suits,"* though it was quite possibly the loudest whisper she'd ever heard.

The girl sat up and pulled her jeans and socks on. "Oh.

Agency. I was wondering when their asses would show up again."

They descended the stairs and Bailey trudged into the foyer, accepting a steaming mug of coffee from Russell with a nod of thanks. She blinked at the men waiting for her.

There were three instead of two.

"Holy shit," she exclaimed, trying not to drop her coffee. "Wasn't expecting to see you."

Agent Townsend's grim face broke into a smile, and at his right and left elbows, Velasquez and Park grinned openly.

"Hello, Nordin," the senior agent greeted her. "I, meanwhile, wasn't expecting to see *anyone* until pretty recently. But I'm back on duty, if somewhat the worse for wear."

She opted not to agree with him, though he did look like he'd aged five or ten years in the last couple of months. He was paler, thinner, and his hair had turned gray in spots, and he seemed to have trouble supporting himself on his legs, but he was alive and functional.

Velasquez added, "We're glad to have him back. You'll be shocked to learn that we need to talk and ask for your help again. There's news."

Park concluded, "And it's bad. I mean, what other type of news *is* there?"

Bailey waved the agents into the living room. "Lemme sit down and get a single mouthful of coffee in me, okay? Then you might as well give it to me raw."

The instant she swallowed, they did.

"Our scanners," Velasquez began, "have picked up staggering numbers of paranormal entities moving across the barrier zones we've established in the direction of our universe. We sent teams in to conduct recon, but half of them vanished, and we had to pull the other half back before they could report on much."

Park asked, "Any of this ring a bell?"

"Sure does," Bailey grumbled. "You probably should have come to me first. Here's what it is. Multiple simultaneous invasion forces from hostile-ass monster races, all of them stirred up by a god who's trying to pull off a coup within Asgard and kick off the frickin' Norse apocalypse. Which supposedly will start a chain reaction of crap that will not spare the Earth. That's the long and short of it."

The three agents were silent for four or five seconds, then a morose-looking Agent Park pulled out a twenty-dollar bill and handed it to Townsend, who slipped it into his pocket.

"I knew it," the eldest agent gloated. "There was no way Bailey would fail to hit peak critical mass in terms of her fucked-up ability to attract unlimited shitstorms of fuckery and myriad bullshit. Judging by the accelerated rate at which every single thing she's been involved with has been worse than the one before, I had no doubts whatsoever that this time, it would be the end of the world as we know it. That twenty was mine *yesterday*, Park. Today is simply the day the inevitable transfer took place."

Park muttered something in Korean while Velasquez snickered and looked at his tablet.

Bailey took another swig of coffee.

"Yeah, yeah, fuck off. Anyway, I can help you in a manner of speaking, but it's gonna have to be on my terms, and you're gonna have to bring your own gear and firepower. I'm already dealing with this stuff on my end, along with the other gods, so it'd make more sense for us to incorporate you guys into our plans instead of the other way around."

The three exchanged emotionless glances, and Townsend said, "Fine."

"Okay. We'll figure out the details momentarily. First, did you find anything useful? Your equipment honestly is about as good as half of my magic. On a good day, anyway."

Velasquez pulled a chair closer to her and set up his tablet on the end table. "We did. Here's one of our screens that plots the energy signatures of supernatural beings on the move. Things were relatively quiet this morning, but right before we arrived, we got a bunch of activity spikes here. Does this place look familiar?"

Bailey blinked at the display; it took a second for her brain to process the crude lines of the landscape relief, along with what looked like multiple smaller buildings inside a segmented wall with towers at its corners. Blobs of light converged on the complex.

"Oh, *fuck*," she gasped. "It's the academy—the training grounds. There were still some students there, last I heard."

After she'd left the five survivors in the castle, she'd told Loki and Balder about it, assuming that one of them, or their subordinates, would render the necessary aid. She still felt guilty for not double-checking herself, and there was no time to ask around Asgard about it. If anyone was still trapped there…

The werewitch guzzled the rest of her coffee and pulled her boots on with one hand while pulling out her phone with the other. She texted Roland, telling him to get

Dante and anyone else he could muster and to meet her here.

Then she turned to the agents. "You guys packing heat?"

Park snorted. "Of course."

"In fact," Townsend elaborated, "we brought the *big* guns this time. To be safe."

"Good," said Bailey. "Agent Townsend, I dunno if you're up to it, but we need all the warm bodies we can get for a potential rescue mission. *Now.*"

Townsend stood up, his legs trembling. "Let's say that it'd be better to put me in the rear. But I'll come."

"Told you!" Velasquez exclaimed.

Park, scowling, fulfilled his end of the bet and went out to fetch the weapons. Bailey followed him, concentrating on the academy and then opening a portal to the same place she'd entered before. As soon as it looked like the agents were ready, she plunged in, not waiting for them to catch up. Besides, it might be better if she scouted ahead.

The werewitch emerged from the astral tunnel into the field directly before the gates of the main castle complex. Things were much the same way they'd been during her previous visit. The place was dead silent, and the castle was still scarred with battle-damage. No hazards or enemies were anywhere in sight.

Bailey jogged to the front gate and peered through it, seeing nothing so far. She glanced backward. The three agents emerged from the portal. Once they were clear, she did not close the doorway, but blocked it off from misuse with a heavy arcane barrier.

Making eye contact with the three men, she raised a

finger to her lips. They nodded, advancing without speaking.

Then Bailey noticed the weapons they carried. They looked somewhat like thick silver shotguns, attached via cords to silver packs they wore attached to their belts. Both the arcanoplasm rifles they'd used against the Venatori and the disruptor devices they'd wielded against Callie's clone-spirits had been slightly different. She was curious about what the so-called "big" guns were capable of.

Raising an arm, the girl summoned her sword, the blade flashing into her hand in an instant. She held it up beside her shoulder as she strode ahead.

They entered the gates, examined the outer grounds, and found nothing. Moving through the next set of gates to the inner bailey, they could see that the dome-shield the werewitch had left over the keep was gone, and the crude material barrier the students had set up had been taken down.

Bailey crept closer, squinting. The blockade had been carefully disassembled rather than destroyed, which suggested that the survivors had taken it down themselves as opposed to a hostile entity battering through it from without.

The girl motioned for them to explore around the far side of the keep. The agents nodded and followed her, their rifles held ready.

They'd barely gone seven steps when the ground rumbled with the unmistakable sound of approaching feet and bodies, charging them. Oddly, though, they seemed to be moving from the forest toward a solid section of the castle wall.

Bailey jumped fifteen feet into the air to have a look.

"Shit!" she exclaimed, noting the diverse mass of unfriendly creatures streaming toward them. A faint purplish glow suggested they were using magic, but there was no time to see what. The werewitch allowed herself to fall back to the earth, deciding it was better to stand with her human comrades than to dive-bomb the enemy alone.

Something struck the stone in front of them. It rattled, and dust fell to the ground. Townsend breathed in deeply through his nose and cocked his gun.

All at once the wall collapsed, the stones falling apart in a miniature landslide and the mortar spraying as dust. In streamed a jumbled crowd of too many types of monsters for Bailey to identify them all at first glance, though she did notice an ogre and a handful of dark *alfar*.

One of the elves was obviously a sorcerer since he held up his hand and maintained a purplish translucent shield a yard or so ahead of the front lines.

Bailey had been about to simply hit them with a river of fire, but the shield gave her pause. She could probably blast through it with sheer force. However, it made her wonder if the creatures had enough intelligence amongst them to enact a diversionary ploy, like a sound-masked rear ambush while she and the agents were distracted by the wall breach.

Her second's hesitation allowed the beasts to stream in. Most charged straight in behind the shield, but half a dozen sprinted to each side, looping around to flank the mortals.

Bailey gestured to the auxiliary forces. "Deal with them! I'll take the center."

She advanced sidelong but at speed, making a narrower target of herself as she hefted her sword. She looked to the left.

Agents Townsend and Velasquez aimed their imposing weapons and fired balls of superheated plasma, white and violet-tinged. Each bloomed quickly to the size of a volleyball and the projectiles struck the small flanking group head-on, exploding into a dome of fire that vaporized five of the six creatures at once and drove the last one reeling back, burned and on the cusp of death.

Nice, the girl acceded. *I ought to see if they can spare a couple of those things for the sheriff's office in Greenhearth just in case.*

Then she crashed into the main force.

Her sword cleaved straight down, splitting the arcane shield asunder, and she was past it as it fell away, beheading the elf mage who'd conjured it with another fast stroke of her blade.

Two goblins tried to attack her legs, and she killed them both with a broad lateral swing. Then she unleashed a kinetic blast that drove half the monsters back to the bottleneck of the fallen wall while causing the rest to stumble forward and to the sides, right into the agents' line of fire.

Bailey leaped a good thirty feet off the ground, scanning the area for signs of any other attacks. There were none that she could see or sense, meaning they ought to be in the clear once they vanquished the current band.

As she floated downward, she channeled lightning through her sword, moving it like a hose across the disoriented mass of foes and destroying most of them before they could regain their composure. By the time she landed, only a single badly-damaged rock giant, two *alfar*, and two goblins remained. The agents had incinerated the rest.

The girl's sword made short work of the smaller combatants. The rock creature, bigger and certainly stronger than the others, might have posed a problem in a one-on-one confrontation, but Bailey was too eager to find the survivors among the trainees to bother with a duel. She detonated a small sonic boom in the center of the golem's chest, shattering it to pieces that were quickly lost amidst the rubble of the wall.

Things went quiet. Surveying the area around her, Bailey saw the agents powering down their guns, looking with grim satisfaction at the smoking sludge and white-hot particles scattered across the ground—the only remaining traces of the monsters they'd blasted.

Townsend looked up. "Like I said, we thought it would be prudent to come with proper weaponry."

"*Very* proper," Velasquez added.

Park scowled. "The military doesn't have this stuff yet. Might come in handy, but then again, that creates openings for China to steal it and reverse-engineer it, so maybe it's better kept as one of the Agency's little secrets."

Bailey muttered, "I wouldn't call it little, exactly. Come on, we need to look for any students who might have survived."

They continued around the back of the keep and soon came to a small stone outbuilding that had another hastily-erected and crude barricade over the door.

Bailey approached and knocked against a wall with the

butt of her sword, calling, "Hey, it's Bailey. Anyone in there? It's safe out here. I've got backup, too."

Footsteps moved, and the door opened inward behind the barrier of debris. "Come inside," said a voice. "Sorry about all this."

"No problem. Step back, please." She waved for them to remove themselves to safety while she split the barricade with her sword and shoved the pieces off to the sides. Then she strolled into the structure, Velasquez and Park following her while Townsend stood guard outside.

Within were eleven people, ten of them unfamiliar. Bailey recognized one as the uninjured young man who'd spoken to her before.

"It's you," he greeted her. "We weren't sure if you were coming back. Someone who said he was sent by Loki came a day ago, maybe? He took the most badly wounded away right as other people filtered in from the woods."

She nodded and waited for the inevitable bad news, thinking of the students of Balder's who'd turned on him during their forestry exercises.

"I stayed behind to greet them. It turned out it was about half students of Balder's who had disappeared days ago and half other students who'd come back to check on things. And then…"

The boy's face was drawn with pain and fear, and it was a few seconds before he could speak again. "The ones who'd been with Balder turned on us. They killed two people, then ran away, alerting those *things* that we were still here and defenseless. I don't know why they did that. Who are they working for? What made them betray everyone?"

Bailey wanted to blurt the answer, but she couldn't risk it. The fewer people who were in on the counter-conspiracy against Fenris, the better.

Instead, she nodded and said, "Yeah, Balder said something about that when I found him. He isn't aware of what the hell's going on yet either. We're going to find out, though, I promise you that. But for now, let's get you out of here and back to safety."

CHAPTER TWELVE

Fenris stepped out of the portal and advanced, allowing Carl to emerge behind him before closing the gateway. He nodded at his apprentice, then turned to survey the scene before him.

Under a blue sky filled with white clouds spread an autumnal forest of tall, thin pines interspersed with oaks and maples whose leaves had turned from green to a profusion of bright reds, yellows, and oranges. The trees rose on the slopes of low, broken mountains and hills, and gulches and ravines crisscrossed them, filled with rushing and burbling whitewater streams. Dead brown leaves crunched underfoot, giving off a musty yet pleasant scent that rose and fell on the cool, gentle breeze.

The wolf-father tilted his face upward, sniffing the air and expanding his consciousness throughout the realm to seek the energy signature of his target. He found it soon enough and gestured toward a high promontory over-looking a densely wooded vale.

Carl smiled and followed his master. The two scaled the

slope toward the cliff, their view blocked by the trees and bushes. Fenris conjured a light wind to disperse the carpet of fallen leaves so they could approach in silence.

The pair emerged between two pines into an open space before the angular, moss-carpeted promontory. A figure sat with its back turned to them in front of a dead fire. A single thin wisp of smoke rose from amidst the ashes and blackened logs.

The seated humanoid wore a vest and short trousers of tanned leather and had furry doglike ears along with slender, half-canine limbs to match. A slight movement of his head indicated that he was aware he had guests.

Coyote began, "Hello, Fenris, and your young friend Carl. I'm unsurprised to see you at such an unusual time. When I'm so...vulnerable." He chuckled as though at a private joke.

The wolf-god took one heavy step forward. "Coyote. We have business to discuss."

The trickster god unfolded his legs and stood up, not bothering to turn around. "Ah, of course. That's your curious idiom for intending to kill me and assuming I wasn't aware. Not only did I smell you all the way from the base of this hill, but I've also noticed a distinct stench of treachery on you for, oh, quite some time."

Carl shot Fenris a narrow-eyed look of concern, but his master waved it off.

"So," Fenris intoned, "you were aware it would come to this, and you've accepted that there is no escape. You might as well turn and face me."

Coyote did, his dog-like features preserving a trace of his usual good humor, though his eyes looked deep and tired and ancient. Next to Fenris, he was relatively small and thin.

"Better?" the trickster queried.

The wolf-father moved two paces closer. "Yes. I can see how old you've grown. Immortal or not, time has taken its toll, and we have come to the end of your journey. Being a lord of tricks and boondoggles will not save you this time since you can't simply magic your way out of your predicament. You face a battle in which your victory is impossible."

Carl moved to the side, blocking a section of the slope that the other deity might have been able to escape down if he'd dashed past Fenris fast enough. "Impossible," he repeated. "I like the sound of that."

Coyote only smiled. "Yes, it's true that I'm old, but I might, perhaps, have a few more tricks to play."

Before Fenris or Carl could act, the canid god jumped a yard to the right at the same instant that he conjured a dozen illusions of himself, the thirteen figures moving with such haphazard speed that it was impossible to immediately determine which was the real one.

The ground beneath the feet of the were-father and the scion turned to liquid, trapping them up to their ankles as the clones struck them in the torso and face with fierce blows of fists coated with magical kinetic force.

"*Damn you!*" Fenris growled, sending out a semicircular wave of electricity that engulfed, froze, and destroyed most of the illusions. Carl, meanwhile, shielded himself from further attacks as he struggled to pull free of the melted ground.

Coyote leaped into the air, avoiding the arc of lightning,

and tossed a cascade of icy water and freezing gas downward so as to further trap and immobilize his foes.

Fenris, rather than react directly, detonated an explosion within the cliff. The entire shelf of rock collapsed in a shower of rubble, the wolf-god and the scion falling downward ahead of the frigid torrent. Carl raised a shield above their heads for further protection while Fenris floated aside, aiming to land on a nearby crag.

Coyote flew down and around in a loop. Fenris guessed the trajectory of his movements and struck him with a sudden small but powerful meteor that made the trickster deity burst into flames while also knocking him out of his gentle flight and sending him careening down into the forested valley.

Fenris and Carl landed on the small peak in time to see their enemy vanish amidst the trees below. The scion struck the area with multiple lightning bolts, igniting the dead leaves and pine needles as well as the wood of the trunks.

"There," Carl grated. "*That* ought to teach him to ruin my boots."

A heavy mist condensed over the burning valley, thickening to water, which extinguished the flames and added clouds of steam to the smoke. As the pair descended to re-engage, the moisture formed into lances of pressurized water that shot at them.

Carl dodged two. "Crap. It's always something, isn't it?"

"*Be silent,*" Fenris snapped. He raised his hand and summoned a powerful and concentrated mass of gravitational force in the center of the valley. Trees uprooted themselves and joined chunks of earth and stone to gather around the miniature black hole.

Coyote's cover vanished. Fenris spotted the dog-like god running for a narrow ravine between two hills and instructed his apprentice to harry their nemesis with a shower of projectiles. Carl happily complied.

As they chased Coyote up the ravine, Fenris canceled the gravity spell so that the clumped-up amalgamation of matter at the center of the valley collapsed into a giant ball of dirt, rock, and wood that shook the ground. Coyote stumbled. One of Carl's arcane blasts had wounded him in the hip, and he couldn't keep his balance during the minor earthquake.

Then the wolf-father surrounded him with shield-matter, encased the shields in sheets of rock pulled from the hillsides, and finally created a powerful spear of flaming plasma and diamond, which he hurled through the center of the makeshift prison.

The coffin of rock fell away and Coyote came into sight, resting on one knee, a smoking hole in his chest. "Ah," he panted, looking up with a face contorted in agony, "I was not clever enough after all. But now, Fenris, let us see if you can *keep* your victory."

The strained gasps faded, and the canid deity's face relaxed into a curious expression of peace. He smiled sadly. The color drained away from him, and his body grew hard and brittle, crumbling into a mass of gray ashes and crisp brown leaves that wafted away on the wind. Sparks and streamers of deep coppery red and spruce green rose and fizzled alongside what little remained of his material form.

Fenris slowly balled his big hands into fists. "It is done.

Only one of them remains. Then the entire council will have fallen."

Carl wiped his brow. "Hah! I can't believe we pulled it off. The old mutt put up a tougher fight than we figured. What comes next should be more interesting still, though."

His master turned toward a shadowed corner of a cliff, where he conjured another portal. "Correct."

As the two left Coyote's realm behind them forever, neither saw the slender black-haired figure that watched them from behind a mirrored illusion on a nearby hilltop.

"All right," Bailey began, putting her hands on her hips and shaking a strand of brown hair out of her face, "it's time to go on the offensive. We've knocked down two armies so far, and we can take on another. Those rock giants seem to be the biggest threat for the time being. Our aim is to remove that threat."

The people assembled before her on the back lawn weren't much of an army, though.

The South Cliff pack had assembled its bravos under Will Waldsbach. Half of them looked reluctant to get involved in another battle after losing their friend Scott to the dark elves. There was also a smattering of wolves from other packs in the area, as well as Russell Nordin. Fourteen men in all.

Of the survivors at the academy, most had gone home or to the hospital, but three had volunteered to join her on the next expedition. They wanted payback and to make a difference, and to ensure that what had happened to them at the training grounds would not happen to others again. Among them was Rami, the guy who'd spoken to Bailey both times she'd come to the rescue.

Agents Townsend, Velasquez, and Park were still there, and they'd called for backup, acquiring an extra seven agents armed, like them, with the so-called "big guns" that had performed so well on the training grounds.

Roland had returned with Dante and Charlene as well as a dozen other witches, many of them familiar faces from the fights they'd all been through before.

They weren't very many, but Bailey had something planned that would substantially balance the odds.

Will raised his hand. "I'm guessing these things are, you know, giant and made of rock? What will Weres be able to do against them? We'll fight no matter what, but I'm not sure how much good we'll be against things like that. All we have is physical strength."

"It's okay," Bailey replied, "I thought about that. You guys will mostly be the auxiliary. If they get too close, attack their legs and then their heads when they fall. Or stick to distracting them, moving fast, hit and run, trying to get them to break their formation—that sort of thing."

The wolves agreed, and the werewitch informed them that she had a surprise. An entire regiment of the Army of Asgard had been placed under her command, and she'd be summoning them presently.

Roland gawked at her. "What? I wasn't aware they had an army."

Dante added, "That's awesome. Do they have, like, projectile weapons?"

Bailey frowned. The soldiers she'd fought with before

had relied on their phalanx formation and melee tactics. "Not sure, but I'm about to contact them. I'll ask if they have, I dunno, bows or something."

Velasquez stepped forward and announced, "Our weapons will make short work of those things on an individual basis, so it'll be mostly a matter of keeping them from swarming us."

Bailey allowed the agents, Will, Dante, and Roland to coordinate their specific strategies while she sat down, away from the group, and reached out with her consciousness toward Asgard and Sigfred, who had taken charge of their temporary occupation of the frost trolls' home realm.

His mind opened before hers, and by extension, the rest of the troops' as well. The werewitch spoke to them.

I need you, and soon. We are going on the offensive against the rock giants. Leave men in the trolls' world if you have to, but anyone you can spare should meet me there as soon as you notice my energy signature arriving. If you have any long-range weapons, bring them.

Sigfred's mental voice replied, *We are ready. The trolls have been quiet, and there are other Asgardian troops who can reinforce the platoon I will leave there if need be. We knew this was coming.*

Bailey was relieved; she hadn't been certain they'd be able to come on such short notice. *Thank you, sounds great. See you soon.*

Her next task was to figure out where the hell the rock giants dwelled and open a portal there.

It took ten or twelve minutes of intense concentration. First she recalled the creature she'd fought at the training grounds, the stony behemoth towering over the dark elves and rabid goblins she'd destroyed with a localized sonic boom. She remembered the entity's arcane signature, its smell and frequency.

Then she mentally scanned the known universe for a domain with a concentration of similar signatures. The realms of the dark *alfar* and the frost giants had been located in a sort of ring that extended out from the base of Asgard, and she hypothesized that the stone giants' homeworld would be somewhere in that vicinity.

She was right. Soon, the location of the domain she sought took shape in her mind, and throughout it were patterns of energy much like that of the creature who'd breached the academy's wall.

"Okay," she murmured, then extended her hands to summon a portal that would take them there. The girl had only the vaguest idea of where to start but figured that an area with an especially high concentration of giants made sense. Their king or champion would likely be well-guarded.

A broad purple gateway opened in the air before her. Satisfied and hoping she hadn't screwed up an overlooked detail, she beckoned to her friends to follow her through.

"Be ready," she told them. Then she walked into the gleaming amethyst mass and through the astral void between worlds.

They emerged into a landscape that was almost shockingly pleasant. It was about halfway between grassland and forest, a rolling plain of emerald grass with lone trees dispersed here and there and occasional thickets at lower points where water would have gathered. There were also masses of boulders piled here and there. The sky was a clear turquoise.

About half a mile before them was a broad, gentle rise in the land, not quite a hill, where the trees were larger but less numerous and the rocks more densely strewn. It appeared that the ruins of a stone structure were perched at the top.

Bailey blinked. *Did we come to the right place? This looks like something out of one of those nineteenth-century Romantic paintings or some shit.*

"Okay," Roland said, beside her, "so where are all the giants?"

A faint tremor went through the earth. Nothing serious, but just enough to cause most of the group to steady themselves so as not to stumble. When Bailey looked again at the nearest pile of boulders, it seemed...different.

"Aw, hell," she muttered. "They're probably hiding amidst these things and waiting for us to stupidly blunder into them. Well, *we're* waiting for the Asgardians. So there."

To her consternation, she didn't see them. Not yet, anyway.

Bailey turned to her small force of volunteers. "They should be here any minute. Be patient until they arrive."

Unless, she added to herself, *it gets to be so long that we have to assume it all went wrong and go looking for them. But that prospect is a ways away yet.*

Fortunately, they didn't have much longer to wait. Bailey sensed a disturbance in the air nearby and then saw a broad purple gateway open there. The gold-armored warriors of the Norse gods streamed out in tight formation soon after.

Charlene and one of Will's friends exclaimed, "Wow."

They *were* an impressive sight. In addition to the spears, swords, and shields they'd had last time, around half of the Asgardians also carried what looked like golden recurve bows, which were curiously lacking in strings.

Bailey walked up to meet them, and Sigfred greeted her. "Lady Bailey, good to see you. As requested, I have assembled the majority of the troops who fought by your side earlier. We've also brought bows that fire arcane projectiles for as long as the archers can maintain their magical strength."

"Excellent." The werewitch grinned. Despite the looming danger, she was looking forward to seeing how the weapons performed. "There was a tremor a few minutes ago, so I think we're going to be in combat pretty soon. Form up."

She quickly filled the divine soldiers in on the tactics and abilities of her other allies, and they arranged their forces so that an Asgardian shield wall was the vanguard, with their archers as well as the agents near the front to fire on the enemy. Witches would be kept in the middle for support magic, and the Weres, along with other Asgardian melee troops, brought up the rear.

Another small quake rattled the ground, but this time, it didn't stop after a couple of heartbeats. It continued and increased. Cresting the top of a low hill, they saw a long line of boulders moving toward them that were mounted atop other, larger boulders—the heads and shoulders of a legion of giants.

Bailey raised her right arm, and her sword blazed with light in her hand. "Get ready!"

The rock creatures crested the ridge—hundreds of them, moving slowly and deliberately in a block formation. The ones out in front held jagged pieces of stone, which they hurled at the interlopers.

Before Bailey could try to destroy the hurled missiles or Roland could shield them from their impact, the Asgardian archers aimed their stringless bows and fired a torrent of golden bolts of light that struck the boulders and blew them into masses of hot dust.

"Nice," the werewitch commented. Then, louder, "Shields up! Move together, but *advance!*"

The witches created a dome-like barrier over and around them and moved it alongside the group, who marched forth to meet the enemy. Bowmen and gun-toting agents fired around the edges of the shield, the golden arrows and white plasma fireballs streaking through the clear air to strike the first two or three ranks of the giants head-on. Dozens of the creatures burst into half-molten gravel.

The rest still marched forward inexorably, shaking the ground with their steps. If not stopped, they would crush Bailey's small task force and move on to batter down the walls of Asgard.

Bailey made a decision.

"You guys," she shouted, "keep doing what you're doing. I'm going ahead to soften them up!"

Roland flashed her a concerned look, and she hastily grabbed him and kissed his cheek. Then she launched over the shieldmen out front, charging her sword with every-thing she could think of, and plunged into the middle of the army of giants.

CHAPTER THIRTEEN

The first wave had fallen. Bailey's berserk charge had softened up the stone creatures, disrupting their initial formation, and she'd nuked the middle portion of their lines. The ones out front were picked off by the overwhelming firepower of the Agency's plasma cannons, the magical bows of the Asgardians, and whatever the witches could come up with.

The Weres were antsy; they'd sat out the battle thus far but knew that they might still be called upon to fight the huge and powerful golems at close range. The giants were slow and unimaginative, but their enormous physical power was obvious.

They also seemed to enjoy combat. No hesitation was evident in them despite the masses of their numbers who fell. They were like automatons whose sole emotion was joy in smashing things.

And more of them were coming. For each wave the interlopers destroyed, two more trudged over the horizon from multiple directions.

As projectiles flew, with the agents' plasma guns doing the most damage, Bailey looked again at the distant hill she'd noticed when they'd first arrived. Something about the place suggested a headquarters to her, and she thought she could detect a concentration of magic there.

"Okay," she told her men and women during a lull in the fighting, "you guys advance. Keep doing what you're doing, and hold the bastards off. I'm going to cut toward that place over there. I think their king, or at least a commander, is based there."

Sigfred, Roland, and Will agreed.

Three dozen giants advanced toward them in a wedge formation, and the archers and agents concentrated their fire on its center to split it in two. The remainder of the monsters picked up speed and closed ranks.

Bailey detached herself from the main force in time to see the giants slam into a hasty arcane shield a foot in front of the physical shields of the Asgardian troops, then their gold and steel lances lunged out, doing minimal but nonzero damage to the hulking stone forms. It was enough to slow and wound them until the casters and gunmen could pick them off.

Satisfied that her people could fend for themselves, Bailey dashed off, cutting through half a dozen giants who tried to block her way.

As she hurtled toward the semi-fortified embankment with its ruins and heaps of boulders and massive old-growth trees, her blazing sword cleaved through stone legs and hands and abdomens. Some of the giants died or fell apart. Others merely stumbled, wounded, and the were-witch trusted her allies to finish them off.

The ranks of the giants thinned here. Most of them had been deployed in the titanic horde that marched against her friends and Asgard. She jumped from ridge to ridge, boulder to boulder, or sprinted up the winding path that led up the low hill as necessary.

She knew the king would be guarded. She came to a low, half-crumbled stone wall at the top of the grassy mesa and easily hopped over it, her booted feet landing in a courtyard whose floor was of different colors of quartz and gypsum.

At the center of the space was a strange throne carved into the trunk of one of the biggest trees she'd ever seen. A huge stone giant sat there, though she could see little of him.

He was encircled by his elite guard, six golems who were larger than most of the others and who wore helmets, greaves, and breastplates of metal and crystal. In their blocky hands, they hefted crudely forged metal lances or club-swords of chiseled minerals.

It occurred to Bailey that she did not know the stone giant king's name, but her challenge ought to be obvious enough.

"You!" she shouted. "Face me! If I win, your army agrees to stand down!" She raised her sword, allowing it to glow purplish-white as she charged it with arcanoplasm. Its blade could cut through almost anything like a serrated knife through soft bread.

A low rumbling, grinding sound rose from the throne area, and it took Bailey a second to realize it was the king's voice. "Upstart fool," he quaked. "She has spirit, but kill her all the same."

The guards advanced.

Bailey darted forward, low to the ground, ducking under the first one's mighty but relatively slow sword-swipe. Her blade licked to both the right and the left, severing both his legs. He toppled to the ground, shaking the hill.

Three more surrounded her, two stabbing at her with lances while the third swung his sword in an overhead arc. These creatures were the slowest and least-skilled of the monstrous races, but their strength was incredible. Bailey had little doubt she could avoid their blows, but if she failed, Roland would have to gather what was left of her in a jar.

She dodged the first three strikes, then conjured an expanding dome of shield matter and sonic vibrations that pushed the giants outward and back, throwing them off-balance.

The girl swung her sword three times. With each stroke, the blade sent a razor-edged sheet of concentrated plasma through the air, cutting the giants asunder, their bodies splitting into halves.

The last two elite guards assailed her. She jumped over the first one's sword and perched on his shoulder, severing his head with a quick strike, only to catch the second's lance in the center of her body.

Bailey saved her life at the last instant with a kinetic cushion that crushed the tip of the lance but also blew her backward. She flipped head over heels and landed hard at the base of an ancient tree. She gritted her teeth as leaves wafted down. Then she was back on her feet, not seriously injured.

The final guard charged her with his lance, his impassive stone face oddly livid with a primitive mixture of bestial joy and rage. He feinted, then stabbed as she dodged, his speed and dexterity noticeably a cut above that of his peers.

But it wasn't enough. Bailey wheeled around the broken-tipped spear and cut it in half, then severed the giant's arm with another upward swipe. His fist came toward her, but she threw a concentrated blast of water into his chest, knocking him back and filling his cracks with water. When she froze it, the expanding ice put enough strain on the fault lines in the stone creature's structure for him to fall apart in chunks.

The king stood up and glared at her. The giants' faces barely had features, yet somehow it was possible to perceive expressions on them and emotions in their glinting quartz-like eyes. She suspected the monarch was regarding her with a mixture of loathing and respect.

Suddenly he was on top of her, having summoned a dormant ability to move his staggering bulk at speeds she would not have expected. His enormous fists bore down on her shoulders. Her sword fell to the ground, and her eyes bulged in shock.

She strained against him. She had the magical strength of a goddess on top of the greater-than-human might of a lycanthrope, but the sheer weight and gravitational force of the giant king was a match for her. Their limbs trembled with the effort.

Then Bailey fell between his arms so that he stumbled forward while she sprinted past him and grabbed her sword. She could see Roland watching her from near the front lines of the main battle.

The king stood back up straight. "No time for this," he rumbled. His hand twitched, and the ground split open beneath Bailey's feet.

Before she could rocket upward from the trap, heaps of earth piled in atop her from the sides. In a second or two she would be buried alive, crushed beneath the matter of the hill.

She forced dirt and rubble first from her face and head, then from the rest of her body with a hasty shield. Then she extended and widened the impromptu crevasse. The giant king fell into it beside her.

He raised his arms to try a counterspell, but Bailey detonated a sonic explosion around herself, pushing away all the debris and flying upward to freedom. With a stroke of her sword, a bolt of lightning as thick as a tree descended from the clear sky and struck the stone monarch's head square on, shattering it into coals and lava.

The girl floated back down to the ruined hill, imagining once again the tendrils extending from her head and heart to probe into her vanquished adversary and drink his supernatural abilities and latent strength.

"Damn," she gasped. Her feet touched the ground, and she reeled and blinked from the hasty infusion of power.

Then she went to the edge of the hill and looked around. To her consternation, the remainder of the rock giants were still fighting her regiment.

And other giants were massing on the horizon.

A tremor of frustration went through her. "What's this shit? Was this guy really their leader?"

As her brain and soul tried to digest the dead king's magical essence, some of his knowledge passed to her, and the answer came to her clearly: No.

There were multiple kings of different stone giant tribes. She had defeated only one of them; the others still had their own contributions to the horde for her to deal with. She extended her vision across the savanna and glimpsed them—four other sub-monarchs were within a mile or so of her position.

But with the new knowledge also came new powers.

Bailey flew back to her allies, her sword raining arcane death upon the crumbling lines of the giants. She landed in front of Roland and Sigfred, her boots treading over a mass of shattered stone.

"There are more kings than one," she reported. "These pricks are a federation rather than a dictatorship, I guess. We need to charge and deal with the rest. The good news is that I think I know how to handle them."

The Asgardian officer just gave a grim nod, but Roland looked at her with a quizzical twist of the mouth. "How might that be?"

She smiled and turned away. "Forward, march. Then watch."

The regiment advanced toward the massed armies of the other tribal leaders. Not only did the already-advancing droves of the creatures come into sight, but still others rose from the earth, assembling themselves from the myriad piles of boulders scattered around the landscape.

Bailey had no fear. Her new abilities were coalescing, and she thought she had a handle on them. Hopefully.

The air split in multiple places as though earthquakes

had happened in the atmosphere, and the ground beneath the feet of the front waves of giants roiled like clouds in a storm. Trees nearby grew taller and sideways, blocking the giants or crushing them with their powerful limbs. Other trees uprooted and fell between the legs of the golems, making them trip and fall. The sky went dark, then brighter again. A few of the giants exploded into clouds of dust.

"Holy shit," Will exclaimed. "Bailey, be careful! You don't want to destroy this whole world."

The girl heard him only faintly, but she knew he was right. The recent infusion from the defeated sub-king on top of all the other magic she possessed was pushing her to the brink of her self-control.

I can defeat all these fuckers, she realized, *and I must be a match for Fenris by now. Unless he has hidden reserves far beyond what I expected, I must have reached his level.*

She calmed the demi-apocalypse that had begun to rip apart the giants, noticing that the monsters had no fear despite the massive losses they'd suffered, and lifted her sword.

"All right," she announced, "let's do this again. *Charge!*"

The tall man stood before the sea, allowing its salt spray and cool, moist breeze to push the hood back from his head and rustle his shaggy hair. His apprentice might have appreciated the sight, but he was not present. The scion had other business to attend to.

The nexus was growing closer. The more they achieved, the quicker they had to accomplish what remained.

Fenris looked down at his feet and the waters beyond. A man could have waded into the ocean for one, perhaps two steps, then the ground would have dropped out beneath him, giving way to fathomless depths that did not seem possible by Earthly standards. There was no gradual slope. Beyond the lip of the sea, it transformed into a downright abyss.

Thus the water appeared a deep cobalt blue, and the sky overhead was covered in equally dark blue-gray clouds. The two shades blended with distance, so the horizon was an indistinct strip of blue-black.

Beyond him was a rolling expanse of barren and dreary heath and bog-tundra. Overhead, a pale white speck of sun was visible behind the cloud cover. It was a domain of nothingness that lay at the farthest edge of the Other.

But it was inhabited.

The wolf-father raised his arms then and began the chant that would call forth Jörmungandr, the World Serpent—the great worm, the devourer, the beast of beasts whose acts would usher in the beginning of the end. Fenris' words echoed across the limitless expanse of cold waves.

And then he fell quiet. There was no reaction thus far, but he knew the serpent had heard his call.

There was someone else he needed to summon, too.

"Thor!" he bellowed, the vibrations of his voice going past the borders of the dimension to reverberate through the halls of Asgard. "Come quickly, for my need is urgent. Death and destruction are upon us, but we may be able to halt them. Come to my aid!"

While he waited for the god of war and thunder to manifest, Fenris turned again to the waters and saw the sea churning and bubbling from a great disturbance below its surface. A vast shadowy silhouette was visible amidst the waves.

He addressed the unseen presence. "Jörmungandr. The time has come at last for you to fulfill your destiny and slay Thor Odinson, your prophesied enemy since the dawn of time. When he is gone, you will be free to swim across the entire universe. Complete the task, for Ragnarök is nigh!"

A deep, almost subsonic rushing sound filled the air. The World Serpent had heard and understood.

As Fenris walked up and away from the shore, they both waited.

A moment later, thunder rumbled, and a bolt of lightning fell from the clouds. When the flash faded, Thor stood on the gloomy heath in full armor, his red-bearded chin thrust forth, looking around for the source of the threat. He gripped Mjölnir in his right hand, the weapon's head resting on his powerful shoulder.

"Fenris!" Thor bellowed. "I've come. What's the trouble? We've had enough goings-on lately, all the border skirmishes and attempted invasions. I'm tired of leaning on the girl and letting her do our dirty work. It will be good to crack skulls again. Point me in the right direction!"

The wolf-father stared at the boisterous deity with a somber, neutral expression. "I'm afraid it isn't that simple, my friend. The border attacks are part of a much larger conspiracy, which we must confront by subtler means."

Thor frowned and spat in the sand. "Bah! Deviousness

and treachery and plotting again. Very well, who are the conspirators? Once we've found them, I will *end* them."

Fenris explained, "I have reason to believe that the unrest of late is the work of the gods of other pantheons. They feel Asgard has grown too strong at their expense, so they have riven us with internal dissent, forcing us to fight the rebel creatures within our own realms as they move to initiate Ragnarök. They are willing to tolerate the destruction this will cause as long as it deposes us."

"Oh, ho!" The thunder god scoffed. "Wretched bastards! We'll intercept them before they get very far with such a boondoggle. Once we've found the *nithlings* who planned all this, I will wring their necks."

Fenris had turned and begun to walk back down from the low heights of the heathland back to the bleak and sandy shore. Thor, still ranting and blustering, followed. The vast dark-blue expanse of the World Sea was before them.

"And having mashed their bones to a paste with my hammer," the red-haired deity continued, "I will dispense the liquid residue of all the mead and ale I've drunk on what remains, drenching them in a veritable yellow shower of—"

With blinding speed, Fenris pivoted and struck Thor with his fist, the blow massively enhanced by a pulse of concussive force. The thunder god careened past the shoreline and landed amidst the churning waters with a loud splash.

The wolf-father intoned, "Jörmungandr! Arise and end it now!"

Thor righted himself and floated magically at waist-level in the sea, not hampered by the weight of his hammer. "What the devil?" he sputtered, water streaming from his beard. "Is this your idea of a joke, Fenris?"

The wolf-god had not intended to answer, but before he would have had time to, the World Serpent showed itself.

Thor spun away from Fenris toward the gargantuan bulk that rose from the depths to tower before him, filling half the sky. Fenris watched, totally still, transfixed by the spectacle.

An expanding wave of water gushed outward as the World Serpent reared its head and neck.

It was like a great finned snake with glossy black and dark green scales, and tendrils trailed from its huge, fanged, dripping jaws. It was larger than any other creature in existence, so big that most minds could not comprehend what they saw. It blotted out the pale and pitiful disc of the sun. The spines on the back of its neck were lost in the low dismal clouds.

Thor's eyes bulged wide in horror as he realized—at last and too late—the awful trap into which he'd fallen. Fenris could *see* the gears of his mind turning, his recollection of the prophecy, his quick and hopeless calculation of how much chance he would have against such a monstrosity.

But the god of thunder was nothing if not courageous. He hoisted his hammer in the air and lightning struck it with crackling fury, making it glow. Thor bellowed a war cry that echoed across the waves.

Jörmungandr responded in kind. Its roar drowned out

Thor's, rendering it insignificant by comparison. Fenris smiled in triumph.

The war god plunged toward his adversary through the waves. Before he struck a single blow, the World Serpent plunged down with a speed and force that created a wind, its mighty jaws open.

Thor disappeared between the creature's rows of fangs as the ocean exploded, white spray rising like a mushroom cloud as the monster bore the god beneath the surface. Then both of them were gone.

Fenris raised his hands and face to the sky, a brief tremor of emotion running through him. He had succeeded. He'd destroyed every last one of the council gods. Some turbulence out in the water suggested the struggle was not yet over, but it would be soon. Thor was too stupid to fight fate.

The wolf-father turned away and walked up the shore to the heath, enjoying the mental image of what had happened before he opened a portal and left the World Sea behind.

Though Fenris did not know it, this time there was no slender black-haired figure watching him from behind a holographic mirror. Unlike his confrontations with the other gods of the council, this was no illusion.

CHAPTER FOURTEEN

Bailey leaned on her sword, breathing heavily and watching over her friends as they rested and recovered from the long, brutal battle. No one had died, for which she was beyond thankful, but many had been wounded or rendered delirious by blows to the head or sheer overexertion.

Once the werewitch had acquired full control of her new powers, she had been able to use them judiciously, turning the environment of the rock giants' homeworld against them to devastate vast numbers of their hosts.

But her abilities had their limits, and she began to tire from the strain, both mental and physical. She'd rested near the center of the formation, helping with magic as needed but allowing the casters, Weres, agents, and Asgardians to do the bulk of the mop-up fighting.

Then they'd met the next of the stone giant kings. Since there were several of them, Bailey didn't bother fighting them in duels but destroyed them outright through overwhelming magic. She feared she wouldn't be able to handle trying to absorb the powers of them all, so she only drained two.

That was more than enough. She'd nearly lost consciousness toward the end of the battle, her mind spinning within her head and her body writhing and trembling. Roland and two werewolves had taken her aside and stood guard over her while the rest battled on.

Finally, she recovered and vanquished the last of the giants with a surge of earth magic that shattered them all. Quiet then set in.

She wondered if this were all of them—if she'd wiped out an entire species. It was a disturbing thought. None of them had tried to surrender. They had plowed dumbly ahead, seeking to do harm to her friends, her allies, her world. She hoped they had children somewhere who would live on but grow up to be smarter than their parents had been.

Roland came up and held her. They did not speak but simply enjoyed the warmth of the mutual embrace, resting their heads against one another's.

After what felt like about ten minutes, a portal opened and Bailey perked up, her hand going to the hilt of her sword. She partially relaxed when she saw Loki step out, but she noted the haste in his demeanor and the nervous look of worry on his face.

Uh-oh, she thought.

"Bailey," the trickster god began, "there is serious trouble afoot, and I'm not sure how much time we have to avert it. I've been working with the other gods, helping them put up resistance to Fenris' assassination attempts while collaborating on the final illusions. He believes at this point that he has killed all of us save one."

Roland waved his hand and asked, "You mean, all but Bailey?"

"No," Loki went on, "all but Thor. That's where things may have gone wrong. Fenris may succeed in destroying him."

Bailey stood to her full height. "Got it. How the hell did that happen? Not that it matters, I guess. Where is he?"

Loki's fingers twitched, and his eyes darted around. The girl couldn't recall having seen him so flustered.

"He is at the World Sea of Midgard, which lies at the utmost edge of the Other. Somehow, either Thor stupidly forgot to tell me that he was answering a summons from Fenris, or Fenris proved cleverer than we'd thought and blocked any message that Thor might have sent. The thunder god is a poor illusionist but a great fighter, so even without me, he might have simply overcome Fenris and driven him off. The problem is that Fenris is not his opponent."

Bailey's gut roiled. She wasn't sure why, but the ominous tone of the mischief lord's words had evoked a primitive and superstitious fear in the depths of her being. "I don't like the sound of that."

"The sea," Loki explained, "is the home of Jörmungandr, the World Serpent, which is quite possibly the most powerful entity in existence, besides the higher gods. These species you've fought are as nothing compared to it in the hierarchy of monsters."

Roland slapped his own cheek. "Jesus H. Christ, Loki, can't you bring us good news for once?"

The deity paid him no heed. "Jörmungandr is another son of mine, but let's not get into that. The important thing is that the prophecy of the End has decreed that the World Serpent's slaying of the thunder god is one of the events that will bring Ragnarök upon us. If we make haste, we might be able to avert it."

Bailey lifted her sword. "Lead the way. I'll rally the troops who are still able to fight."

"No," Loki protested, "they cannot fight this creature. They'd only die uselessly, providing fodder for its hunger and fuel for its coming rampage. You must go alone. It's risky, but you and Thor together might be a match for the serpent."

The girl frowned, and another shudder of primal dread struck her. "Fine, I'll do what I have to do," she stated. Then she thought of something. "What if Fenris is still there? Won't it blow our cover?"

The god of mischief closed his eyes and shook his head. "It can't be helped. He'll likely flee if he sees you, or lie and say he was trying to help Thor when Jörmungandr appeared or some such nonsense. If you must confront him now, so be it. We will come to your aid. But first, you have to save the lord of storms and battle. Go!"

He turned, not waiting for a response from her, and opened a rather crude and ragged portal with a hasty swipe of his hand.

Bailey hugged Roland, and they shared a quick kiss.

"Come back," the wizard instructed her.

"I will." She ruffled his hair, then dashed into the glowing gateway, ready to fight destiny itself.

The shoreline was bleak and cold. It was nothing like the sorts of beaches people went to on vacations. Rather, it reminded Bailey of the ends of the earth, which in a fashion, it was. The Other ended here. What, she wondered, lay beyond?

The waters stretched past the horizon, deep, treacherous, and as blue-black as a clear night's sky in summer.

The girl looked around. There were footprints in the sand, but nothing else. Fenris was nowhere to be seen; that, at least, was a relief.

But Thor was not in sight either, nor was there any sign of a giant sea-snake.

"Dammit, Loki!" The werewitch sighed. "Did you finally crack under the pressure and make a mistake? Am I in the right goddamn place?"

She hoped not.

The other possibility, of course, was that she was too late. That Thor had already been devoured and the sated serpent had moved on, pursuing whatever unholy business came after its killing of the thunder god in the sequence of the prophecy.

And she was tired. She'd recovered somewhat from the lengthy struggle against the stone giants, but she needed a proper day off. Still, there was nothing she could do for the moment.

She tried to draw energy from the realm as Coyote had taught her, but the section of the Other beside the World Sea had hardly any vitality to offer. It helped a little, but not much.

There was a splash far out in the ocean. Bailey squinted. The waters were roiling and bubbling about half a mile in front of her and off to the left. Rolling waves appeared at the spot and moved toward the shore. Bubbles rose to the surface, and whitewater crashed into the air.

The girl hoisted her sword and levitated twenty feet into the air, intuiting that she'd need to be mobile.

"Shit," she groaned.

The sea split and erupted. A colossal black shape, serpentine and hideous, burst from the waves, its size momentarily confounding Bailey's ability to perceive what she was seeing.

Jörmungandr looked somewhat like a typical snake, somewhat like a limbless Chinese dragon, and somewhat like a nightmare abomination that had no analog in anything she'd encountered. The sky was half-filled by its head and neck alone, so the creature had to be *miles* long.

It whipped its head around and opened its jaws, revealing a throat like a cavern and fangs the size of trees. From its mouth, an object emerged as if thrown or spat. It spun toward a lumpy promontory above the beach, and it took Bailey a second to realize that it was a humanoid figure.

Her eyes bulged, and she jetted toward it. As it drew closer to land and she drew closer to it, familiarity set in. The figure was a burly man with salt-soaked red hair and beard and armor stained with brine and blood. A short yet mighty hammer was clutched in his fist.

"*Thor!*" Bailey cried, picking up speed as she flew laterally toward him. She couldn't tell if he was alive or dead, conscious or not.

Behind her, the World Serpent let out a deafening, air-splitting, and disturbingly high-pitched roar, the kind of earth-rending shriek she associated with *kaiju* films, though stripped of any semblance of charm or camp. Here, with the world's most powerful monster right before her, the sound was terrifying.

Bailey conjured a lattice of thin strands of moving air and shield matter, making a magical net where Thor was about to land. He plowed into it and slowed but still crashed into the ash-colored cliff with more force than she would have hoped.

The girl halted her advance, allowed her feet to touch the ground, and ran to the thunder god's side. "Thor! Are you all right? Talk to me!"

The red-bearded deity twitched and rustled, spitting water out of his mouth. "Yes! Bloody hell and damnation. Is that Bailey? Curse Fenris for this! Help me stand."

Bailey put her arms under his shoulder and slowly raised him to his feet. She examined him at the same time, grasping that he had nearly drowned, been severely banged up, and had taken a further battering from his impact with the cliff, though not as bad as it would have been without Bailey's net.

As the thunder god regained the ability to stand, both their gazes drifted to the ocean. Jörmungandr was swimming toward them, its tunnel-like maw hanging open and its flat, cold, hideous eyes staring at them with hatred and hunger.

Bailey asked, "Can you fight? I can, but—"

"Yes!" Thor growled. "Not as well as I'd like, but that drooling worm hasn't beaten me so quickly. Side by side!

We should have rid the universe of this beast long ago, I say."

Staring at the abomination bearing down on them, Bailey wondered how many gods would have been a "safe" number to attack it.

I'm guessing about a dozen, she surmised, *as a conservative estimate. But we'll have to make do with two, or more like one and a half.*

Then again, is this fucking thing really any worse than an entire army of smaller critters? Hundreds of elves, trolls, and giants are nothing an H-bomb-style explosion can't solve.

"Okay," she told Thor, "shield your eyes and yourself."

She thrust her hand toward the serpent and nuked it.

The air, land, and sea all turned white as a sphere of pure fiery death erupted at the point of Jörmungandr's upper throat. Together, Bailey and Thor conjured an intensely powerful shield around themselves as shockwaves of force, heat, and overtaxed sound rippled past them, devastating the area. They closed their eyes.

When they opened them again, much of the land had turned black, and the sea was a couple of feet lower. So much of the water had evaporated that the brief slopepoint between land and water's edge was gone; there was now a lip of land that plunged into the watery abyss.

Jörmungandr still lived. It blinked, and smoke rose from its scales, then it glared at them with a fury that made Bailey want to turn around, run, and pretend none of this had ever happened.

No, she ordered herself. *We don't do shit like that. We stand and fight, no matter what.*

"Bah!" Thor roared, waving his hammer. "Come on, then! Let us tussle with this thing like men!"

With a long howl that faintly resembled a cheer or a laugh, Thor launched into the air, straight toward the lord of monsters.

Bailey sighed and followed him, her sword at the ready.

Jörmungandr's head, the size of an apartment building, snapped toward them, its motion creating a wind. It wasn't even moving all that fast, the girl realized. It was so big that it didn't *have* to.

She thought of how easy it was for her to reach out and squash a tiny bug that was desperately scurrying at top speed away from her, and she shuddered.

Thor wheeled around, narrowly dodging the biting strike of the serpent, and his hammer whacked it in the chin. Sparks crackled from the point of impact, and the monster's head jerked aside enough to suggest that the blow had had *some* effect.

But not much.

Bailey had dodged the attack by shooting upward and in the other direction, and she swung her sword at the side of the serpent's neck as she flew past it. The blade, to her horror, bounced off the creature's scales like a nail file against plate armor.

What the fuck? She was on the verge of panic, and since she rarely panicked, that scared her still more. *This sword can supposedly kill gods. What in the name of all the worlds is that thing?*

But the impact of Thor's hammer had done more than nothing, so it wasn't invincible.

However, Thor had faltered and stumbled after his

successful strike. His wounds had reduced him to fifty or sixty percent of his normal fighting ability.

Bailey flew into the air, trying to think of what might hurt the beast as she kept a close eye on its movements. It seemed more interested in Thor than in her.

The thunder god bellowed and launched a stream of lightning at it. Jörmungandr twitched, and its movements became irregular. The bolts didn't exactly stun it, but they interfered with its ability to attack.

Bailey breathed, "Okay, then." She commanded the clouds overhead to discharge a sequence of six columns of lightning, five of which struck the black serpent directly. The sixth landed in the sea and electrocuted the water enough that it likely contributed to the effect.

Jörmungandr squawked in a way that rattled the pebbles on the beach. It froze in place for a second or two, then it shot a hateful glance at Bailey. It turned back to Thor, but a huge loop of its body crashed out of the ocean to whip toward the girl.

She dove away from the gargantuan coil, wondering if the monster's apparent susceptibility to electricity had to do with it being an elemental creature of water. Perhaps it was something more mundane.

Thor and Bailey began a game of cat and mice, each of them harrying the abomination with concussive blows or lightning bolts, trying to wear it down as it thrashed and snapped at them with movements that could have leveled half of Greenhearth.

Soon, though, the World Serpent started to demonstrate intelligence. Rather than attack them with its body, it attacked them with huge waves of water, which also absorbed their lightning strikes.

And each time they were disoriented, it moved in for the kill with its hideous jaws. Bailey noticed venom dripping from the fangs.

Thor called, "Don't let it swallow you either! It tried to do that to me. I lodged myself in its throat until it had to spit me out, but if the beast gets you down its gullet, you'll never get back out."

As if on cue, Jörmungandr snapped its mouth toward the thunder god, who barely escaped the fate he'd warned against. Instead, the side of the serpent's lower jaw bashed into him and sent him splashing and rolling back onto the shore.

Bailey threw lightning at the dragon's eye to distract it for a second as she rushed to Thor's side once more.

The red-bearded deity was weaker still. "Bailey! I'm having trouble lifting my hammer. Link with me, and I will give you a portion of my power so that you can heft it."

She frantically recalled the lessons of Loki and Fenris on how to share magical ability between deities and an invisible siphon-tendril emerged, locking into Thor and establishing a conduit with him.

A surge of strength entered her, and it made her want to fight. It was like a rolling storm within her heart.

Jörmungandr was bearing down on them again.

Bailey let out a loud war cry and seized Mjölnir, imbuing the hammer with an entire storm's worth of lightning and then hurling it straight into the serpent's face. The weapon ricocheted off the beast's nose and lips, lighting its face with flashing sparks, and it trembled in pain, immobilized.

The hammer flew back, landing in Thor's hand instead of Bailey's, but the thunder god's infusion had given her an idea.

"Thor," she said, "lightning hurts it more when it's out of the water, and it can't move as fast, and I think our whole problem is those damn scales. If I can slip my sword under one, I might be able to drain some of its strength and give it to you, and then we can barbecue it with the biggest thunderclap in known history."

Hope and vitality flowed back into the heavy, bearded face. "Ha*ha!* That might work. Let us try then."

They linked arms, Bailey helping Thor move as they levitated, coming eye to eye with Jörmungandr. Thor hurled his hammer again. It moved in an irregular pattern, striking the serpent's chin despite its attempt at dodging, though it landed with less force than Bailey's blow had.

Still, it was enough to stun the monster for a second or two. The werewitch moved them around the side of the creature's head, and they planted their feet against its neck. Bailey found the edge of one of the huge black scales and inserted her sword's point beneath it, then stabbed hard.

Jörmungandr tensed, and she knew it was about to throw them off. The sword was little more than a pinprick to it, but it still represented a breach in its defenses.

"Thor!" she exclaimed, "help me hold the sword!"

"Aye!" he agreed. One of his big hands closed around the handle beside hers. As the earthquake-like force of the monster's sudden whipping of its neck threatened to dislodge them, their combined strength held them in place.

Bailey began to steal Jörmungandr's essence, funneling it not into herself but into her companion. The effect was instantly noticeable, and the werewitch could feel her share of the burden diminishing as Thor drove the blade in still deeper.

The girl cast a quick spell to fuse the flesh beneath the scale to her blade, then she shouted, "Up!"

Both gods gripped the hilt, wrenching upward with the full reserves of their respective divine strength. Jörmungandr, shrieking horribly, resisted with its considerable physical might, yet somehow the two humanoid deities prevailed. The serpent was slowly dragged upward, more and more of its unimaginably huge body emerging from the sheltering waves into the open air above the sea.

Thor raised his hammer. "*Lightning!*" he bellowed. "Power of the storm—of *all* storms—come forth! Bailey, help me invoke it. We need as much as we can imagine!"

Thunder crashed around them, and white flashes appeared in the roiling dark clouds overhead. Soon, despite the World Serpent's intense thrashing, the clouds began to close around them like a dense bluish fog.

Bailey struggled to hold onto the sword and control the wrenching movements of the monster, but she spared as much of her willpower as she could to aid Thor's spell. She spread her mind across all of the Other, seeking out every neutron and electron of power she could find and bringing them all to the point of their battle.

Sparks and bolts leapt through the clouds around them, and the flashes became more frequent, to the point that they resembled a strobe light.

Jörmungandr, its primeval brain grasping what was

about to happen, bellowed in fear and rage and committed its full strength, enough to split the world asunder, to trying to break free of the sword and the deities who held it.

Bailey's mind was stabbed with a note of panic as she almost lost her grip. She had to abandon the lightning conjuration in order to focus everything she had on not letting go.

But it was too late for the serpent. Thor had control of the storms that were his purview, and Bailey had done her part by channeling half a dimension's electricity to where he could use it.

The wrath of the heavens was unleashed. A column of lightning a quarter-mile across fell from on high, striking Jörmungandr square atop the head. At the same instant, a thousand other bolts struck the beast across the half of its body that was exposed above the World Sea. The electrical energy coursed through its form and reacted violently with the water where the other half was still submerged.

The werewitch screamed in pain and Thor did likewise as both struggled to repel the incredible power surge that threatened to leap through the sword into their forms, overloading them.

But they held firm, finally withdrawing the blade from the serpent's neck once its death scream faded and its colossal body went limp.

The flashing lights in the clouds faded as Jörmungandr fell, its head and neck flopping sideways to impact the ocean below in a mile-long line. The sea exploded, and a tidal wave rose from the impact, flooding and over-whelming the shore. After some moments, the waters retracted, and the ocean was once again calm as the World Serpent sank forever into its unfathomable depths.

Bailey and Thor drifted earthward from the sky, landing on a blasted hill a quarter-mile or so back from the water's edge. Pools of black water lingered in low places around them, left there after the great wave receded.

Despite the dose of stolen strength Bailey had given him, the thunder god did not look good. Bruises were visible everywhere there was exposed skin, and the non-bruised parts of him were pale and sweaty. He also seemed to be succumbing to severe exhaustion.

"I'll live," he assured her before she could ask. "I've had a bad day, you might say, yet it was also a *great* day, was it not? We defeated the monster said to be nigh undefeatable!"

He laughed, though the sound transformed into a cough. "My wounds are merely from the pounding it gave me. I escaped its fangs. The prophecy stated that I would overcome and slay the monster but be bitten and die of the venom. That isn't what happened. We have defied destiny."

The girl blinked as the magnitude of what he'd said sank in. "Shit. Not bad. I suppose that means we can also defy the End of the World."

CHAPTER FIFTEEN

Loki, to his credit, responded to Bailey's summons within about forty seconds.

He took her and the thunder god in at a glance, dismissing the portal behind him and surveying the now-scorched heath that abutted the World Sea.

"What in the universe happened here?" he marveled, wrinkling his nose at the smell. "Did you conjure up a forest and then burn it down?"

Bailey scowled. "I tried to nuke it. The World Serpent, I mean."

"Oh." Loki sighed. "Well, I'll assume it didn't work, yet both of you live, so you must have done something right."

Thor raised his head. "Indeed. We live, and Jörmungandr does not." He wheezed and fell back into semi-consciousness.

Bailey locked eyes with the lord of mischief. "He needs help. He's gonna make it, but you can care for him better than I can or get him to those who can so he can recover his strength. Right?"

"Yes," Loki confirmed. "I will stabilize his condition myself—beyond what you've, er, attempted—and then take him back to Asgard for further healing."

"Good." She scowled again. "How come you couldn't help us fight that thing? I'm amazed that two gods were enough to take it down."

The trickster deity knelt beside Thor, not looking at the girl. "As I mentioned previously, Jörmungandr is—or *was*, pardon—one of my children. Confronting it myself would have caused complications I don't wish to discuss at the moment, and it's best if you don't ask again. Or think about it too hard."

The werewitch decided to drop the issue. "Okay, fine." She briefly wondered who, or what, Jörmungandr's mother might have been, then instantly blotted the thought from her mind.

Loki performed a couple of healing spells and Thor fell into a cozy slumber, though he still looked weak.

Bailey just breathed in and out, watching them. For the moment, she felt warmth, peace, and relief. She wanted it to last and had no desire to risk plunging herself into further chaos, and strife, or uncertainty.

But her desires were less important than her duties. "All right," she inquired, "What do we do next?"

It occurred to her that she probably sounded tired and scared. It *also* occurred to her why: because she *was* tired and scared.

Ever since we learned about Fenris' plans, she mused, *we've had to rush around in a constant state of worry and anxiety, wondering what he's going to try next and never knowing when or where the next domino will fall. I'm getting sick of it. I just want to face him down and put an end to this once and for all.*

But it was impossible to say how she would deal, emotionally, with the final confrontation. She'd been trying not to think about it too hard.

Loki calmed her somewhat by giving her a straight answer.

"Next," he began, "you should head to the realm of the *draugar*. The undead, as I believe you people rather crudely refer to them. They've marshaled their forces near the boundary between their realm and ours, and, well, you know the rest. It's much the same as with the dark elves, frost trolls, and stone giants."

Bailey tilted her head back and groaned. "Goddammit. How many armies does Fenris have? It's like he's turned the whole universe against you guys. Against us, I mean."

Loki held up a finger. "Not all of it. Only a fraction, albeit a rather significant fraction. But you should make haste. Things have proceeded far enough that the draugar lords may provide the last distraction Fenris requires. If they make any progress, Asgard will have to divert its forces to confront them, potentially leaving my son open to perform the ritual that will bring about the end."

"Noted," Bailey responded, inhaling and steeling herself for the battle to come. She wondered when she'd get time to rest again.

The god of mischief went on. "There is one other thing to note. We are quite confident that Fenris considers the best-case scenario to be sacrificing you in his stead to bring about Ragnarök and then rule over the ensuing wreckage, but there is something that remains nebulous to us. He *may*, if he pushed to utmost desperation, decide to trigger the Beginning of the End according to the original prophecy. In other words, sacrifice himself after all, simply to destroy Asgard and the cosmic order that depends upon it. Thus, even in death, he would be victorious. After a fashion."

The girl's blood went cold. "Does he hate you guys that much? Why would he do that?"

Loki shook his head, and his eyes and the lines of his face were drawn and sad. "I do not have the answer to either of those questions. As I said, it's uncertain. He might be willing to surrender if he fails to sacrifice you. There's only one way to find out, isn't there?"

She sighed and nodded. "Yup. Okay, how do I get to the draugar's world?"

Loki clapped his hands, and a doorway of shifting, glimmering amethyst light appeared before him. "That way," he stated. "Call your Asgardian regiment and have them join you. I will locate your other friends and provide portals for them as well."

The werewitch stepped toward the gate, then remarked, "What would I do without you, Loki?"

He shrugged. "Fail, most likely."

"Yeah, yeah," she grumbled. "Whatever. Thanks, though."

Bailey stood at the head of her regiment. A few of the Asgardian troops, the Weres, and the witches had been rotated out due to injuries, exhaustion, or shellshock.

Townsend also needed to recover, given his weakened constitution and bad leg, but the Agency had sent an extra four men to more than compensate, and Asgard had dispatched an additional platoon of soldiers to further swell her ranks.

The world in which they found themselves was perhaps the least pleasant place Bailey had ever seen, with the possible exception of the dark *alfar*'s homeworld. That realm could claim, if nothing else, to a sort of austere desert majesty.

The homeworld of the draugar, by contrast, was like a scene out of a nightmare. The landscape consisted of frozen swamps and tundra swept by a bitterly cold wind so vile that Bailey had had to draw upon the powers she'd gleaned from the frost trolls to protect her people and herself from it.

Low, jagged mountains the color of dark ash streaked across the bogs, resembling broken ribcages. Diseased-looking trees rose here and there. Bones were scattered throughout the icy morass. The worst thing, though, was the greenish sky through which black clouds raced. Bailey tried not to look at it.

The draugar themselves, thus far, had been no match for the combined forces of Earth and Asgard, let alone the goddess of witches and Weres. Hundreds of their corpses were strewn about, adding to the grotesque morbidity of the environment. The humans watched them warily as if half expecting the undead they'd slain to rise a second time.

They remained still, however. The only movement

came from the occasional wafting of ice fog from the frozen marsh-pools.

Bailey addressed them all. "Okay, we've kicked the shit out of them so far, but next up is storming the castle over there. Once again, I want you all to let me do the heavy lifting out in front. I'll clear the path, and you secure it while watching my back. From what Loki told me, no draugar will fight without being ordered to, so they ought to collapse back into neutrality once we take out their leaders."

Dante quipped, "Oh, wonderful. We won't have to fight an entire planet's worth of assholes like we did with the rock giants."

Velasquez checked his plasma cannon for the little light that indicated it was done recharging, then cocked it, putting it back into fire mode. "Exactly. I'm honestly starting to get sick of this crap."

Park pouted. "I'm not."

"Shut up, Park," the senior agent snapped. "Maybe it should be you and Bailey alone who handle all of this."

He nodded. "That would make sense since I have the second-highest kill count after her."

Bailey waved a hand. "Yeah, true, though it's a pretty distant second. Enough yakking. Sigfred, you ready? Forward!"

Once again, the Asgardian troops formed the core of the second line of defense, while the Agency's men provided the main secondary offense. Bailey charged across the valley toward the shale-colored, gargoyle-decorated structure that rose from the nearby foothills.

Corpses in rags or armor or greenish robes rose from

nowhere to attack them, and Bailey could see, hear, and smell legions of other draugar massing beyond the crags, slowly converging on the structure where their leaders waited.

The werewitch carved through them, and they went down easily under the heavy fire of plasma balls and enchanted light arrows, not to mention the plethora of spells summoned by the witches.

Lycanthropes were able to participate in the current fight as well. Though hordes of them made a distinctive rustling sound, an individual draugar was disturbingly quiet and could easily sneak up on the regiment, launching a sudden attack with its ability to expand its size and strength or distort its shape. At those moments, it helped to have wolves ready to pounce.

Bailey conjured a wall of flame and pushed it into the front of the undead castle, slowly doing a sweep of the structure's face, melting or incinerating most of the draugar who might lay in ambush.

"Come on!" she urged her allies. She charged across the stone bridge to the front gates, her sword ready.

What followed was a tense and difficult alley-fight as the Earthling-Asgardian force struggled through the labyrinthine halls of the gloomy keep, barely evading traps or constant ambushes as the leering, hissing undead sprang from every shadowed cranny.

They came to a staircase that wended up to the top floor, and there Bailey sprang into a broad, dusty, crypt-like chamber.

Before her were five stone chairs arranged in a semicircle, their occupants facing her. She beheld a quintet of draugar in green and black robes finer than those of any others they'd encountered.

Bailey turned to Roland and Sigfred. "Hold the door," she instructed them. She could hear more rustling footsteps ascending the staircase. Then she advanced toward the ruling council of the draugar.

In the central chair sat a dead woman with taut blue skin and ragged, wispy hair. She raised a bony hand.

"Have you come, Bailey Nordin," she asked in an eerie whispering tone, "to challenge us? Fenris warned us you might."

The girl pointed her sword at the councilwoman's face. "I have unless you agree to call off the invasion."

The five exchanged stiff, glassy-eyed looks. The woman in the center rasped, "We do not. Die, Bailey Nordin. *Die.*"

The speed with which the council members sprang from their seats came as a surprise, considering the unnatural stiffness of their movements and the fact that two of them had been cobwebbed into their chairs.

Worse, Bailey felt her knees wobble and her arms drop. The sword's blade trailed against the floor, she couldn't move, and fear and nausea overwhelmed her.

The corpses were advancing, essentially floating toward her at top speed.

No, she decided, it's psionic bullshit. Magical fear attacks, mind-over-matter propaganda trying to convince me I'm too weak to lift my damn sword and so forth. It'll take more than that to beat me.

She scarcely shook it off in time. The lead councilwoman was upon her, the bony fingers inches from Bailey's face.

The girl swung her sword straight upward, imbuing it with heat and light, and split open the dead woman's chest. She fell back, letting out a hollow scream that seemed to originate from someplace other than her body, and fell to the floor, brittle and withered.

Then Bailey spun, shielding herself from the next psychic assault as well as blasts of ice and attempts to conjure poison within her bloodstream. Draugar magic was cruel and insidious, but she'd faced stronger.

While her friends fought off the drones who came up the stairs toward them, Bailey struck down the remaining four members of the ruling council, draining some of their power with each kill. The unnatural and vile aspects of draugar sorcery made her want to throw up, but her mind was adaptive, and she made herself appreciate its subtlety.

The sounds of combat ceased. Once she got herself under control, Bailey walked out of the main chamber and found her allies staring dumbfounded at a host of corpses that did nothing but stare back.

"Well," Roland observed, "it worked. Without their leaders, they've reverted to being, uh, dead people, I guess."

Charlene cringed. "They're still *standing*, though."

Bailey issued an order. "Sigfred, get your men's shields up and advance. I'm guessing you can just push them aside."

Her estimate proved correct, and their uncanny foray into the realm of the walking dead became an exercise in absurdity as slack-jawed corpses were bowled over, knocked against the walls, or trampled underfoot. Once they were safely out of the claustrophobic confines of the castle, the Earthlings all burst out laughing, though the Asgardians remained stoic.

"Man," Velasquez commented, "that was, like, night and day."

Bailey nodded. "We stopped the entire draugar rebellion in one fell swoop. Mission accomplished."

She tapped into her reserves of magic to create a dome of protective heat and a mist of healing essence within it. Everyone sat or leaned on their weapons, resting after the fight.

Roland came over to Bailey to check on her. She suspected she didn't look so good, and the wizard helpfully confirmed her suspicions.

"Yeah," she muttered. "I'm getting tired, not gonna lie. And draugar magic is probably the worst I've had to absorb, in terms of how...*palatable* it is."

He frowned and put his arm around her shoulders. "I see. What I'm curious about is, would you say they're more like zombies or vampires?"

The girl shrugged. "Neither, really. Zombies with more intelligence or vampires with less sex appeal, maybe."

"Fascinating," Roland commented, and she could see his eyes going distant as his intellectual curiosity turned to the subject of undeath.

While he was preoccupied, Bailey reached out with her mind toward Loki. She needed to tell him that the job was done, and he needed to tell her what came next.

I imagine, she pondered, *that it all comes down to how far along you-know-who is in his plans.*

The throne room within the high palace of Asgard where Odin had once reigned was again occupied, though no one sat in the great chair.

Carl the scion was there, directing the students from the academy whom he and Fenris had turned to their cause, and who would act as their disciples, helping them with the final preparations.

"You there," he announced, standing with hands on his hips at the base of the throne, "ensure the altar is perfectly centered in the chamber. It's possible that the fundamental forces of the universe won't care, but why risk it? Besides, Fenris likes a job well done. Oh, and the rest of you, work harder."

Grumbles went around the chamber.

Then purple light spilled into it from the corner, and out strode Fenris. Everyone rose to their feet, facing him.

Carl greeted him first. "Welcome back, my lord. We're nearly done with the second tier of all the divine red tape. I take it Thor is worm bait?"

"Yes," Fenris stated. He continued his slow, heavy walk toward the base of the throne where Carl had been and turned to address the whole group when he reached it.

A moment went by, then the wolf-father's eyes, hidden beneath his hood, passed across the faces of all his acolytes.

"My children, my devotees," he began, his low, gravelly voice growing louder and more resonant, "we have entered the ultimate phase. Everything is now in place for the last act we must perform in order to reign over a new world."

Heads nodded, and subtle currents of excitement went around the chamber.

Fenris raised a hand, moving it in a slow wave. "All

the arrangements have been made. The monstrous peoples have absorbed most of the wrath of the gods and their new champion, and those of them who remain will act as our soldiers in the campaigns to come. That same champion of Asgard who shall be offered up in my stead will soon come to the sacrificial altar of her own free will.

"I shall reign over the next eon. Carl will sit at my right hand, and the rest of you will sit at my feet, learning what you'll need to act as my ministers and heralds. The authority of the old gods will no longer impede our advancement.

"But there are some who might still oppose us. The rank and file of Asgard for one, though they are oblivious to what is truly happening. They won't understand until it is too late, but their defeat is assured. There is also—"

The doors behind them were blasted inwards, and the illusions that Fenris had conjured to divert suspicion from the throne room melted away. A shining sword's blade lashed out and carved through the barrier he'd raised, and in strode a single figure.

"—there is also *him*," Fenris finished. He lowered his hand.

Tyr, the god of justice, leadership, and contracts, stood amidst the usurpers, his sky-blue eyes bright with right-eous fury.

"How dare you!" he pronounced in a voice that rever-berated like a gong. He was tall and dark-haired, chiseled and muscular. He resembled Balder somewhat, though darker and more careworn, with a greater air of harsh dignity about him. He wore silver armor and carried a shining longsword with a crossguard that resembled the wings of a white bird.

Fenris replied, "How? It matters not *how*, but I *do* dare."

"Silence!" Tyr shot back, and the trumpet blast of his voice made the acolytes flinch. "I know all. The depths of your treachery have been revealed to us, Fenris. Here you gloat as if in victory, when in fact, this is the moment when you reap not as you wish, but as you have sown. Such is the destiny of traitors."

Fenris was silent and stared back at the angry god with a perfectly neutral and unflappable expression. "Oh," he finally said. "I had no idea."

The lord of justice drew his sword. "You lackeys, stand back. Fenris! Face me in single combat. You do not deserve a trial or tribunal, for your guilt is known to all. I am here to carry out the execution. You will die by my hand."

The wolf-father reached up and slowly pulled the hood back from his face, exposing his craggy features and ragged, graying hair. "Executioners," he pointed out, "only kill those who are incapable of fighting back." He gestured at his students. "And we all are firm believers in standing up for ourselves."

The man standing before the throne was no more. A huge dark shadow streaked across the chamber, piling into Tyr in a frenzy of fur, fangs, and claws.

Carl laughed. "He actually thought we were going to just stand here and accept his judgment? Amazing."

Tyr bellowed in rage as he and Fenris struggled, the justice god's sword prevented from slaying the wolf-beast by the heavy paw against his arm. Tyr rallied and tossed Fenris back.

Before he could strike, one of the acolytes stepped in and stabbed him in the side with a dagger a hand's breadth above the hip.

Screaming in fury, Tyr pivoted and swung his sword at the man's head, dropping him instantly. Then Fenris was upon him again, and so was Carl. And the others.

"Bastard!" the god of justice protested. "You would violate the sanctity of single combat? Cowards!" Claws raked him, knives slashed his limbs and torso, and Carl pummeled him in the face and groin with his fists.

Fenris, speaking with the terrible growl of his true form, replied, "The end of all things is upon us, Tyr. That includes foolish traditions of chivalry."

Carl twisted Tyr's arm, and his sword clattered to the ground.

The wolf-father's jaws snapped down over the justice god's wrist, biting off most of his arm below the elbow.

"Hah!" Carl scoffed. "Release him. For the moment."

The acolytes backed off as Tyr staggered back in pain and shock, the stump leaking ichor on the floor as their master chewed and swallowed the severed arm. Then Fenris looked at one of his students.

"My son," he rumbled, "finish him off."

The disciple shifted into a wolf the size of a large bear with fur the color of tarnished bronze and pounced at the maimed deity.

Tyr ducked the attack and fled.

"Vengeance!" Tyr barked as he retreated through the doors, his boots clattering down the halls of the palace until he emerged from its central keep. "You cannot escape justice, Fenris! Your time will end."

Carl, watching him leave, suggested, "Hmm. I bet he goes to Bailey and tells her to come here, exactly as we planned."

Fenris, abruptly back in the shape of a tall, hooded man, made a fierce grasping motion. "Fan out. Disperse all forces not loyal to us. I will call the auxiliaries. Lock this place down; we must have it under total control. Remember, Bailey is now as powerful as I am, and she's coming."

CHAPTER SIXTEEN

The girl envied her friends. They'd all been allowed to go back to Earth, if only temporarily, or to Asgard in the case of the divine regiment.

On the plus side, the council chamber had an aspect of its atmosphere that relaxed and refreshed her more than she would have expected. Possibly more than a good night's sleep and a nice meal at the Elk, in fact.

"Loki," Bailey asked, "how's he doing?"

The lord of mischief had propped Thor up in his seat amongst the thrones in the great crystalline room. The other deities were not present, so seeing only one of them sitting in his place, and him wounded and foggy-minded, was downright weird.

Loki answered, briefly touching Thor's face, "He's improving. Still somewhat below where we'd all like him to be, however, and there are no healing arts of which I'm aware that will speed up the process."

Bailey grimaced and leaned against a pillar. "So, what's our timeframe? For him healing up, *and* for Fenris annihilating the universe. I'm kinda hoping the first one happens before the second."

Without looking at her, Loki remarked, "Aren't we all? Such things are never certain, though. Thor, are you there? You are the one most affected, so what do *you* think?"

The god of war and thunder opened his eyes. They were bleary, but he recognized the locale and his company.

"Ah," he mumbled, "it's likely I won't be my old self for another day or two, as mortals reckon time. That might not be soon enough to intercept the bastard wolf-mutt."

Loki frowned. "We cannot wait that long. Tyr has finally moved, and all the pieces are in place for Fenris to make his final play."

Thor nodded. "If he's moving to the last phase of his scheme, I fear I won't be of much help to you. A weakened god falling on his face during the big brawl would be more of a hindrance than anything."

Bailey's abdomen tightened at the thought of having to take on Fenris and his allies without a full complement of greater deities to back her up, but she understood.

"Yeah, you're right," she admitted. "We don't want to lose you, and by surviving the attack of the World Serpent, you already threw a wrench into Fenris' plans."

Thor reached out, and Loki helped him to his feet. The pair trudged closer to the girl, who stepped forward to meet them halfway.

The thunder god was still carrying his hammer. He raised it to chest height.

"Bailey," he began, "not so long ago, I tested you to see if you could lift Mjölnir. You could, and with me unable to fight, I'm giving you my mantle for the time being. You shall carry my hammer and my powers. Not forever; that is impossible, for Mjölnir must always return to me. But I can, we'll say, loan it to you."

Loki raised his eyebrows but said nothing.

Bailey hesitated, then reached out and accepted the great hammer. A flash of lightning filled the chamber, but there was no roar of thunder to accompany it. Once more, the girl felt like a storm of courage had welled up within her.

Thor smiled. "Now, if only temporarily, you are the goddess of werewolves, witches, *and* thunder. Ought to be useful. Wield my powers well, and don't drop the hammer off the side of Asgard or anything stupid like that."

She had to laugh. "I won't. Thank you, Thor."

Loki aided the red-bearded deity in returning to his chair, then faced the girl.

"It's time," he stated. "With Thor's little gift, you should be more than a match for my fool of a son. Send word to your friend back on Earth that the hour has come to retake Asgard and save your world, ours, and all the others in between."

Roland stood in the town square of Greenhearth, Oregon, which Sheriff Browne had begrudgingly closed to out-of-town traffic for the time being. It was a nice day that felt to him like the beginning of autumn, though when it came to seasons, you could never be sure.

"So," he began, his gaze scanning the crowd. Agent Velasquez stood to his right, holding a plasma gun, and to his left were Will Waldsbach and Dante Viari. Just in front of him and slightly off to the side were the three Nordin brothers. "I hate to sound like a politician two months before the election, but I am once again asking for your support."

A half-dozen chuckles and an equal number of groans went around the group.

"Bailey is going to need all the help she can get," he continued. "The mere fact that so many of you have shown up is encouraging, but we'll all need to fight as well. This is no longer only about the fate of Weres or witches, or about Greenhearth, or Portland, or Seattle, or any other specific place. This is about the fate of the universe. Hard to believe, I know, but anyone who's willing to join us…"

His voice trailed off as something caught his eye. Amidst the mass of witches who'd crammed themselves into the square, one was moving forward, squeezing between others. He glimpsed an unpleasant shade of fuchsia.

"*Holy shit!*" the wizard shrieked. He threw a massive shield in front of him and then, in a continuous sweeping motion, turned, grabbed Velasquez's plasma gun, and dived for cover behind a trash can. "Everyone get back! *Fire in the hole!*"

Once safely hidden, he gradually rose from behind the waste receptacle, gun held ready in trembling hands, peeking over the top of the bin.

Nothing had happened. The square was totally silent, and everyone was staring at him. He ignored them, his gaze singularly focused on the skinny young woman who'd made her way to the front and center of the audience.

Shannon DiGrezza cleared her throat. "Um. Yeah. Hi, Roland." She flipped her neon-purplish-pink forelock away from her face.

He stood up, his mouth making random, undignified movements as he attempted to speak. "What the *hell* are you doing here?" he sputtered eventually.

Velasquez, looking disgruntled at having his weapon taken from him, asked, "Who's this, your ex-girlfriend?"

"*No!*" Roland barked instantly. He took a deep breath. "No. This is Shannon. She," he coughed, "is an old acquaintance of mine from Seattle."

Velasquez shrugged. "Give me back my gun, or you'll be charged with forcibly disarming a federal agent."

Roland pressed the plasma cannon back into the agent's arms without looking at him as he staggered three steps forward.

"Look," Shannon said, "this is extremely unpleasant for both of us, okay, but I actually came to, you know, help you out here. I heard what's going on." She folded her arms across her chest and looked sidelong at nothing in particular. "And I also came to, um, apologize."

It took Roland another twenty or thirty seconds to respond. "Okay," he gasped. "That's not what I was expecting, but I appreciate it. Anyway, assuming—no offense— that this isn't just a ploy to get close to Bailey and murder her before kidnapping me, we can always use another talented sorceress on our side."

The witch's jaw dropped. "*What?* How could I possibly *not* take offense at that? I am, like, *debasing* myself by coming here to say I'm sorry, and you—"

"Okay, okay." Roland held up his hand, palm outward.

"Sorry. I counter-apologize for saying that part. Otherwise, uh, yes, I'm sincerely glad to have you as part of the team."

Shannon gritted her teeth but nodded, then melted back into the crowd, allowing Roland to complete his motivational spiel.

He was distracted, though.

Out of all the things in the universe I considered LEAST likely to happen, he marveled, *we ended up with an apology from Shannon. If there was ever a time to believe in miracles, this is it.*

Bailey stood on the broad avenue near the center of the city of Asgard, atop the sacred mountain that hovered above the clouds. The divine army was assembled before her, Sigfred and his regiment and two other units of comparable size as well.

An Asgardian chamberlain elaborated upon the situation to the werewitch. "The enemy's lackeys somehow launched a sneak attack from within the palace. Many of us were slain, and our forces were driven across the Rainbow Bridge. We have no friends upon the floating palace; it is entirely within the evil one's clutches. The fighting men you see here are all that remain to us."

The girl nodded, trying to suppress a pang of guilt at the notion that they should have moved sooner. "Who and what all does he have on his side?"

The chamberlain explained that most of the opposing forces consisted of the very monsters they'd been trying to keep away from Asgard's lower borders. No one knew how a combined army of the creatures had appeared at the pinnacle of the divine realm.

"Okay," Bailey told the Asgardians, "I have reinforcements on the way. Once they arrive, we'll retake the palace and put a stop to this."

Everyone's head turned toward the sound of rapidly approaching footsteps. A figure jogged down the marble streets toward them, a tall man in silver armor with a thick makeshift bandage of torn cloth wrapped around the stump of his right forearm.

The chamberlain gasped. "Lord Tyr! What has happened? Were you caught in the palace??

Tyr, seeing the assembled strength of his allies, slowed his pace.

"Yes," he replied in a voice like a deep-toned bell. "This is all the work of Fenris and his treasonous disciples. They mean to initiate Ragnarök! Demigods, scions, and ascended proto deities from the training grounds are with him, and he is the one who inspired the monstrous peoples to rise against us. I had feared it might be too late to strike back."

Bailey gave a grim smile. "It isn't. Tyr, I've heard of you, but we haven't met. I'm Bailey Nordin, the new goddess of Weres and witches, temporarily sitting in Freya's place on the council. I'm expecting anywhere from, uh, thirty to a hundred reinforcements from my world. That includes lycanthropes, witches, and operatives of the US government who have extremely big guns."

The god of justice's strained face relaxed, and he swelled with renewed confidence. "Good. I have heard of you also, Bailey Nordin, and I have faith that we may yet achieve victory."

The girl sent her mind toward Roland, catching his attention and telling him telepathically the whereabouts of Asgard so he could open a portal and bring the rest of their army to her. She noticed that he seemed flustered and distracted but figured it was because of the magnitude of the battle they were about to enter.

Moments later, a purple gateway appeared in an open area in the square, and Roland strode through, followed by thirty elite agents including the three they knew well, as well as nearly a hundred Weres and witches.

Sigfred nodded. "Impressive. We have more allies than we thought, though the numbers of Fenris' forces are still greater."

Bailey went over to her fiancé and put her arms around his neck, planting a kiss on his lips. "Welcome to Viking heaven," she said.

"Good to be here." He gave her a quick, discreet squeeze and hastily said, "So yeah, let's get moving, might as well get on with the fight as soon as—"

Bailey looked over his shoulder at the group of witches who had accompanied him.

"*Holy shit!*" she exclaimed, jumping back and summoning her sword to her hand. "Everyone get back!"

Roland closed his eyes and rubbed his temples. "It's okay, dear. I already had a talk with her. Shannon apologized—no, really—and wants to help. I, uh, wasn't sure how you'd react."

The werewitch stood staring at the fuchsia-haired

sorceress, whose face was glum and irritable, but nothing in her demeanor was hostile, not exactly.

Bailey exhaled and lowered her sword. "Okay. I guess I can accept that as true."

Shannon stepped forth. "It is. After the last time we met, and, um, like, after I heard about what happened to Aida and Callie..." she blew a puff of air up from her lips that knocked her forelock away from her face, "I just, I dunno, felt like holding a grudge would be a waste of my time."

Bailey blinked. "Yeah, I think you were right about that. Well, if you're sincere, then welcome aboard. This ain't going to be an easy fight, though."

"*Obviously*," Shannon shot back. "I'll do my part."

The girl nodded and then greeted everyone else who'd shown up: her brothers, Townsend, Velasquez, and Park, Will and his pack, Alfred, the shaman from farther south in Oregon, and his pack, Dante, Charlene, and a witch named Mavis whom Bailey recognized as having helped them against the Callie-clones, and many others. She thanked them all.

Then the leaders conferred on formation, marching orders, and overall strategy. The rough plan was to do something similar to the tactics Bailey had used against the monsters in their homeworlds, with the Asgardian shield wall out front and agent's guns and witches' spells providing the artillery, while Weres covered backup and ambush defense. Naturally, Bailey would be in the lead.

Tyr approached the girl. "Bailey, allow me to offer you a portion of my powers to carry with you into the fight. I too am a god of war in the sense of strategy and command."

He placed his remaining hand on her forehead, and she envisioned the tendrils of magic running between them. A small but potent infusion of divine authority entered her being, and she felt more confident than ever. The shapes that the battle might take seemed clearer.

The god of justice stepped back and spoke to everyone. "You will need all the strength you can muster to assail the palace and defeat Fenris. I, therefore, will remain behind and guard Asgard against any incursions through the lower borders. It is the least I can do."

Bailey thanked him and asked if he'd be all right.

"I can manage," he told her. "Go."

The chamberlain gave them his blessing, and the small but powerful and motivated army of Asgard and Earth moved down the avenues of the divine city. Civilians peeked out at them from windows and alleys.

Bailey, out in front, held Balder's enchanted sword in her right hand. Strapped to her back and waiting to be drawn with her left hand if needed was the hammer of Thor.

Sigfred was close behind the girl's elbow. "The evil one's followers seized control of the far side of the city after they took the bridge. We must plow through them and then retake Bifröst, which will not be easy."

The werewitch nodded. "So be it."

The good news, she saw, was that Fenris' lackeys were prepared for a siege, not a pitched battle or urban warfare. They were tightly packed near the arch that led to the Rainbow Bridge and had not endeavored to spread through the streets. Clearly, the girl concluded, the goal was simply to delay her until Fenris could complete his ritual.

But, she recalled, *doesn't he need me for it? What if they're trying to lure us in, kill everyone else, and take me to be sacrificed?*

The muscles along her jaw tightened. They wouldn't take her alive.

Her division marched into the relatively open space before the archway and the bridge, where the horde of monsters attacked at once. Their numbers were at least as great as those of Bailey's allies, and she knew Fenris must have far more on the bridge or in the floating palace complex.

"Shields up!" she yelled.

Stone giants hurled giant boulders. Dark elves fired their bows. A pair of frost trolls flung ice orbs like the ones they'd launched from their catapults. Draugar mages cast spells of fear, cold, and poison, which Bailey and Roland intercepted while shields both material and arcane reflected the physical missiles.

The archers of Asgard retaliated with their bows of light, and the agency's troops fired their deadly plasma cannons. A handful of *alfar* mages conjured barriers that blocked some of the projectiles, but others got through, striking monsters down by the dozen, turning them into piles of burning death.

Bailey raised her sword. "Hold your positions! I'm going forward." Then she charged.

She drove a wall of electrified water ahead of her, noting how much stronger her lightning magic seemed since Thor had empowered her. She watched as it swept hostile creatures aside or wounded or paralyzed them, leaving them easy prey for her singing blade. Bodies dropped.

The stone giants tried to crush her between them. She responded with an expanding kinetic burst that shook one to pieces and drove the rest off the edge of the mountainside, so their huge blocky bodies tumbled and vanished in the sea of clouds below.

Behind and around her, her allies kept up their own careful offense, picking off the enemy with well-placed attacks. Bailey summoned a whirlwind of burning plasma around her and plunged into the thickest part of their formation, incinerating them with her mere presence.

How, she wondered, *did Fenris get all these fuckers up here? He must have taken direct control of them via a treaty with their kings, and now they're running on his orders, no longer subject to the authority of their own leaders.*

She kicked aside a goblin, decapitated an elf, disemboweled a troll, and skewered a draugar. The carnage was horrific, but the enemy refused to surrender. Soon all but a handful of them were dead. The Asgardians took the remainder prisoner and shuffled them aside.

Bailey caught her breath and checked on her side's casualties. A few Asgardians, one agent, and one witch had died in the battle. Several others were injured. No one she knew well had fallen, but it pained her to think they'd be unable to win this fight without losses.

She looked at the bridge.

Half as many monsters were stationed along its shining translucent length as had guarded the arch, but they were crammed into a far smaller area. The girl also saw snipers waiting on the walls of the palace. Even with shields, they'd be heading into a potentially deadly bottleneck.

She had an idea.

Bailey pulled Mjölnir off her back. "Lightning!" she cried, and bolts fell from the clear sky to illuminate the hammer's head. With a battle roar, she flung the weapon straight up the bridge.

It spun along Bifröst's length, sending out lightning bolts at random in every direction as it moved. The first lines of the enemy were dead before they could grasp what was happening. The rest, seeing the fate of their comrades, turned and ran.

But the hammer was faster than most of them. Smoking corpses fell in waves before the magical weapon's advance. It destroyed three-quarters of the host before the final quarter plunged through the palace gates to relative safety.

Bailey summoned Mjölnir back to her hand before it could enter the palace since she didn't want it to destroy the place. Then she motioned for her troops to charge.

They did, moving at a jog up the seemingly insubstantial causeway. Mortals in particular looked uneasy, doubting that a bridge made of light could support them, but it held firm beneath their tramping feet.

Halfway across, the snipers began firing. They seemed to be dark elves shooting arrows that had been enchanted with various spells, giving them greater damage potential and some ability to penetrate arcane shields.

The witches devoted their magic to renewing barriers that faltered under the barrage. Meanwhile, Bailey and the Asgardian bowmen shot down half the arrows with careful blasts of their own. Finally, they picked off the snipers, and

Bailey destroyed them with homing fireballs while they tried to flee or seek better positioning.

At last, they reached the palace gates, finding them shut and barred. Bailey didn't like the thought of destroying such beautiful architecture, but their circumstances were too dire to worry about that, and she could always help Asgard rebuild. She powered up her sword with an intense charge of arcanoplasm and split the gates with a strong vertical swing.

As the combined Earthling-Asgardian force hustled into the front palace courtyard, they saw that the battle had only just begun.

At the head of a host of monsters supported by four demigods in hooded coats not unlike the one Fenris always wore was a familiar figure: an athletic, dark-skinned young man, smirking at the new arrivals. In his hands, he carried a steel mace much like the one he'd used to engage the werewitch in friendly fights at the training grounds.

"Hi, Bailey!" Carl greeted her as his allied archers and bombardiers readied their weapons. "You should not have listened to stupid, unimaginative gods like Tyr and Thor and Thoth. And especially Balder, whom I personally shot with that accursed arrow, in case you hadn't figured that part out yet. *They* are the *real* problems in our universe. They're holding everyone back."

The girl glared at him across the shining marble steppingstones and closely cropped emerald grass. "Fuck you, Carl. I knew you were a traitor already, but thanks for admitting it for everyone else to hear."

Rather than wait for him to react, she fired a massive plasma beam at his face.

Carl launched himself upward at blinding speed, and the blast vaporized a dozen or more elves, goblins, and draugar behind him. Then the next phase of the battle was on.

Fenris' forces began using hit-and-run tactics, harrying the sides of the formation with their weaker units while especially large stone giants and elite elven mage-archers pressed them with suppressive fire. The other four demigods unleashed a flurry of spells, but Roland alone was a match for any of them and was able to neutralize most of their attacks.

Carl was nowhere to be seen. Bailey tried to control her anger and hurt. She recalled the good times she and the scion had shared at the academy, and the knowledge that it had been a facade made her burn with vengefulness.

But she had other things to deal with.

One of the other hooded demigods attacked her with a miniature hurricane of acid and a flechette storm of random chunks of sharp stone and metal. The girl summoned a form-fitting shield around her and bulled straight through the attack, renewing the shield matter as needed and boosting its deflective properties until the demigod was struck with some of his own debris.

He tried to flee, but Bailey threw her sword like a javelin, impaling him, then summoned it back to her hand to engage a squad of dark *alfar* swordsmen.

Meanwhile, Roland was grateful to have Shannon contributing to the battle since she'd always been a fairly talented witch. Her distinctive fuchsia bolts of lightning still made him uncomfortable on a primal level, though.

Dante and Charlene worked as a couple, with him

handling defense and her offense, gradually breaking up sub-formations of the enemy or destroying stone giants who tried to hurl magically-augmented boulders at them.

Will and Alfred led their packs in wolf form into the alleys and stairwells of the palace's surrounding outbuildings, hunting down and killing the monsters who tried to hit-and-run the main force. Though fast and stealthy, the elves and goblins were ultimately no match for the predatory instincts of wolves.

Townsend fired his plasma gun from the rear of the group toward flankers, and Velasquez and Park commanded their squads closer to the front. They caught the remaining demigods in crossfires of burning plasma, which proved too much even for semi-divine beings.

Sigfred maintained his men's formation as they slowly advanced, their shields battering aside attackers and their arrows and lances making short work of them thereafter.

But the enemy still outnumbered them, and it wasn't over yet.

CHAPTER SEVENTEEN

Bailey swung her sword again and again in the delirium of combat. As bodies fell around her, she caught sight of the enemy commander at the same moment that a stray chunk of rock giant smote her to the ground.

Carl pointed his index finger at the tight formation of Asgardian soldiers, pantomiming the firing of a handgun, and a white-hot explosion like the detonation of a plasma grenade bloomed amidst them. Dead, burning troops fell in all directions, and their smoking weapons and armor clattered to the ground.

Bailey hurled herself back to her feet, her brain seething with rage. "You son of a bitch!" she howled, tossing Thor's hammer at him.

The scion's eyes widened as he took note of the deadly projectile, and he jumped upward and back, shielding himself from the hammer's profusion of lightning bolts, though the weapon sought him out despite his efforts to weave away from it.

Finally he encased it in a sphere of water that shorted out its electrical functions, then froze the water and used a gravity wave to blast it into a side alley.

By then, Bailey was on top of him. She kicked him in the stomach before he could react to her.

He grunted loudly and flew back ten feet. She moved in on him with her sword poised, though he recovered quicker than she'd have preferred. He lashed at her with his mace, halting the momentum of her charge. The bludgeon knocked aside her sword, though its blade half-melted the mace, rendering it useless for further attacks.

He tackled her, forcing her back against a wall and raising his fist to smash her face in. She was faster, ducking under the blow and jabbing him hard in the kidneys, then kicking him in the back of the knee. He stumbled away, narrowly dodging a swipe of her sword.

Carl picked up a fallen spear by one of the dead Asgardians and swung it at the girl like a quarterstaff. She fought defensively against his first couple swipes, then realized he was slower and weaker than she. He had not powered himself up as she had. He'd been too busy accompanying Fenris on his errands to betray and murder the gods.

"You," he asserted, "have no idea what's in store for you. There's a lot more going on than simply fighting me."

Bailey caught the spear's shaft in her left hand and split it in two with her sword. Then she brought the pommel of her weapon hard into his face, cracking his jaw and cheekbone and knocking him over.

She told him, "Yeah, and you've never been dead, so you have no idea what's in store for you, either."

She was about to finish the scion off when she saw a mixture of blue and golden light taking shape behind him. She hesitated.

Carl stood up, oblivious to the illumination at his back. "What," he grated, though the damage to his bloodied face made speaking difficult, "you want this to be a fair fight, is that it? You could have killed me."

"No," Bailey retorted, looking at him coldly. "I figured I'd let someone else do the deed."

Carl spun at the same instant that Balder's rapier pierced his lower right side and came out of his upper left chest. He spat blood as he looked the god of beauty in the face.

Balder's eyes burned with subtle yet intense anger. "You should not have betrayed us, Carl," he intoned in his soft, pleasant voice. "I treated you as well and fairly as any valued apprentice. Not so with Fenris, who is not as smart as he likes to think. In truth, he was the one who was fooled. You killed none of us. We live on."

With a fast, sharp motion, the deity twisted the blade, then pulled it free while throwing Carl to the ground. The scion's face showed total shock as he stiffened and lay still.

Balder frowned, looking at the corpse. "I am the god of innocence," he observed. "I...perhaps should not have done that, but he shot me with a cursed arrow while hiding. Among other things."

Bailey shrugged. "I'd call it fair, then. Come on, though. It will be good for troop morale to see you up and around."

Fenris stood before the throne of Odin, supervising the ritual. They'd begun the ceremonial magic that would open the way to the next stage of reality, leaving the old world behind in ruins.

Six of his half-god trainees had volunteered to be chained up and used as conduits. They writhed on the ground under the stresses of the dark and potent arcane energies being employed.

"Fear not," he assured them. "When the ordeal is over, you will share in the power that is made available by the cracking asunder of Asgard."

For the moment, though, their role was to function as grounding agents. The forces of darkness the wolf-father was required to channel created surges of excess and harmful magic that could have consumed and killed him. His chained disciples absorbed enough of it to allow Fenris to continue his incantation.

He raised his arms, speaking words so old that the gods didn't know from where or when they'd originated. Visions flashed before his eyes, a primordial string of universes being born and then dying. One door closed. Another opened.

Still the perilous energies swirled and grew in intensity. The throne room was charged with them. The act of diverting the penumbra surges failed to kill his acolytes since they were all part-divine beings, but they would be weak and depleted of magic for quite some time.

But they ought not be necessary. There were only two things left to do.

A pair of disciples, the only ones left in the chamber

who weren't acting as conduits, approached Fenris as he reached the ritual's climax. As per his instructions, they lowered him to his knees, wrapped him in chains near the center of the floor atop the central sigil of the occult pattern he'd drawn earlier and beside the crude sacrificial altar, and put a gag over his mouth.

Thus, at the moment the buildup of dark energies reached its peak, ready to be released with the final offering, he took on the role of the hapless prisoner.

His acolytes faded back to stand against the walls and wait. Fenris stared at the chamber's doorway, which was still open, thanks to Tyr's intrusion. The trap was ready to be sprung.

The girl would come, he knew. He'd trained her himself. In a way, he was proud of her.

Bailey paused around the corner, leaning against the corridor's wall in the brief lull and examining the handful of allies she'd brought with her into the keep.

Roland was there, of course. So was Russell, always the most ferocious fighter among her brothers. Agent Park, who was probably the best man with a gun amongst the feds. A squad of eight Asgardian troops allocated by Sigfred, and of all people, Shannon DiGrezza, who still pretended to look annoyed at "having" to be here, but who had thus far proven her desire to make amends.

"Okay," Bailey whispered, as the sounds of battle raged outside, "he's going to be in the throne room. From what

Loki said, that's where the ritual to end the world has to be conducted. It's down this hall and around another corner. There might be more resistance…"

Shannon made a sharp "uh" sound in her throat. "Great. Why am I here, anyway?"

Roland covered his mouth to stifle a bark of laughter. "You alone can answer that question, I believe."

"Shut up, Roland," she snapped.

Russell glared at her to silence her, and Bailey waved a hand in Roland's face to encourage him to do likewise. Park smirked but didn't comment.

They'd had to separate from the rest of their allies due to an unexpected wrinkle in the plan. After overcoming Fenris' forces in the palace courtyard, a portal had opened in the sky above a high tower and more monsters had streamed in, firing down at them. Others had charged down to harass the Earthling-Asgardian task force.

Balder had told Bailey to go on ahead with a small, hand-picked group while he assumed command of the rest and kept the monstrous host busy.

The werewitch had chosen her team, breached the doors of the keep, and moved in for what she knew would be the last thing they had to do.

Mere seconds after they moved out with Bailey out in front, a force of about a dozen foes appeared around the corner. "Get them!" the girl barked, trusting Roland to shield her as she summoned waves of fire and ice within the hall's narrow confines.

The new opposition consisted of more treacherous demigod-trainees as well as a smattering of hybrid monsters unlike anything Bailey had seen before. One took the form of a bronze-furred wolf and charged them, barking and drooling madly.

The demigods blocked Bailey's magical attacks as the wolf advanced. It bowled past her with surprising speed and made for Roland.

The wizard had been focused on defending against a swirl of plasma spears, and his eyes bulged as the beast pounced at him. Then a fuchsia blast of energy knocked it into the wall.

Roland sighed in relief. "Thanks," he told Shannon, who looked away, then he conjured a sword-like protrusion of silver. The wolf-creature pounced at him again, but this time he fell back and skewered it through the throat, killing it and hurling it aside.

One of the hybrid monsters, a cross between a frost troll and a lizard, bounded ahead and tangled with Russell, but the towering young Were slammed its head into the ceiling and then ripped its guts out.

Park laid down a barrage of plasma fireballs that blew through the trainees' arcane shield and melted one of them into a mass of atoms. The others panicked as Bailey sprang into their midst, but it was short-lived since they all died within five seconds.

One of the half-gods tried to flee into the throne room, its entryway oddly doorless. Bailey threw her sword and it hit him in the back, launching him ahead and pinning him against the far wall, where he hung lifeless.

Her friends moved up behind her, but as she stepped over the threshold into the chamber, an opaque blackish-purple barrier slammed shut behind her, blocking them off.

Shit, Bailey thought.

She had to trust that they'd be okay. Her business lay ahead.

Fenris knelt in the middle of the floor, chained and gagged, an unexpectedly pitiful sight. Eight humanoid figures in hooded robes hovered around the periphery of the room, but they made no move to speak or act, and Bailey let them be for now. The room pulsed and throbbed with a vague, dim light and a subsonic buzzing that the girl recognized as an incredible well of divine power.

She crept to the side of the wolf-father, her erstwhile mentor, forgetting that she no longer had her sword, and looked at him.

What the hell? This has to be a trick, but Loki and Balder never mentioned anything about it.

"Fenris," she said, "are you...okay?"

The wolf-god groaned and raised his head. His dark eyes gleamed faintly within his hood. Bailey reached out and removed the gag from his mouth.

"Bailey," he began, "free me from these shackles. The worst of what I feared has come to pass."

Grimacing, she broke the chains with her bare hands, and he slowly rose to his feet, moving as though he were weak and exhausted from long imprisonment.

She asked him, "What happened?"

He shook his head, the motion slow and regretful. "The other gods have betrayed me, and all of us." He flexed his hands. "They feel we've grown too unruly and are insufficiently grateful to them for their wise leadership."

The bitterness was thick in his tone. "They've secretly stirred up all this trouble, intending to sacrifice me according to the ancient prophecy of Ragnarök and bring about the end of the world. Their long lives have driven them mad, and they'd rather end it all than deal with the imperfections of their followers. I tried to raise a few who might fight against them, but they cruelly destroyed them with their mercenary army of traitors and monsters."

"Goddamn!" Bailey exclaimed. "I had no idea."

Keeping up the act was difficult, mostly in that she could scarcely believe he would lie in such a shameless fashion, but also because it was so hard to believe. It rekindled both her doubt in her course of action and her hope that he might be innocent after all.

What if Loki was the one who set us up? He's a devious prankster and was always kind of a supercilious prick, to be honest. But there's the holographic footage. The confessions. I know they were real. I accepted it, and I'm kidding myself by trying to deny it. Dammit, Fenris, why did you do this? I wanted to—

The wolf-father cut off her ruminations with his coughed-out exhortation. "Please, help me. We may be able to stop it if we act without delay."

"Okay," she responded. "How?"

He glanced around the chamber, which seemed darker than Bailey remembered it. "We must enact a counter-ritual together. Two gods will split the difference of the unleashed energies; neither of us will perish, and that will confound the prophecy. Stand there." He gestured to the spot on the central red sigil where he'd been chained a moment ago.

The girl took her place as instructed.

"Good." Fenris stood beside her. "We can ward each other for protection if any of the remaining deities try to intervene."

Remaining? Bailey thought. *He's aware, then, that some of them are dead. Or so he thinks.*

The wolf-god raised his big, callused hands. "Stand still and wait. Thank you, Bailey. Thank you for *everything*."

As he unleashed his magic upon her, there was a tiny, barely-perceptible change in his expression—a cruel and savage twist at the corner of his mouth.

The goddess of Weres and witches caught the surge of his power, the amalgamation of the dark, destructive energies he'd built up here. She stopped it, blocked it, precluded it. Red and blue sparks and flames erupted between them as her divine might resisted his.

"Thank you," she yelled back, "for *taking your place*, you mean? For putting up with more lies than I can count? For dying so you can do every fucking thing you just accused everyone else of doing?"

The magical impact of her resistance was such that Fenris stumbled back a step. He blinked and gawked, and as the magic threatened to spiral out of control, he diverted it in the form of a dark-purplish bolt that struck the chamber's wall near the ceiling and produced smoke and debris from the impact.

Bailey stepped forward. "I know everything, Fenris, and I mean *everything*. You were the one who set this up. You only trained me, raised me up, freed me, so you could put me up as a sacrifice and get to be king of whatever comes after the end of days. Carl helped you, and he's dead for his trouble. The monsters you duped were defeated. And there's something else I know that you don't: you can't win."

Fenris recovered from his initial shock and stood up straight, towering over her, his eyes lost in the darkness beneath his hood. His mouth was once again grim and unfeeling.

"Perhaps you do know, but you were born a mortal, and you will do what every mortal must. *Die.*"

The man was gone, and the beast attacked.

A monster the size of a house bore down on the girl, its fur bristling and its fangs and claws moving in for the kill. Its eyes glimmered with psychotic fury. The low animal cunning it had relied upon was cast aside and only the creature remained, reverting to its natural tendency toward pure, mindless destruction.

The girl shifted to meet him. She grew instantly to the same size as her opponent, confronting him for the first time as a beast of matched and equivalent power. Their forelegs lashed at one another; their foaming jaws snapped at eye and throat and belly. Awful snarls and howls filled the chamber.

As they locked together, wrestling and thrashing, ripping and clawing, another battle took place contermi-nously with the physical one. Their magical wills clashed, striving against one another, with neither able to win a clear advantage.

Levels of arcane and divine force that could have sundered or repaired whole worlds smote and crackled.

Fenris attacked the werewitch with all the wild energies he possessed and the primordial powers of destruction he'd invoked.

The girl retaliated with the knowledge and might of the other gods and with the things she'd learned from them or from the many peoples of the universe. Everything from the subtle elemental lore of the frost trolls to Coyote's instruction in the finer arts of hand-to-hand combat returned to aid her.

The noise and furor of their battle echoed and shook the walls. It was likely obvious in its terrible wrath to anyone in the floating palace.

Fenris growled in both physical and mental forms, *"Aid me!"*

The eight disciples advanced from the walls brandishing daggers and swords, ready to wound and distract Bailey to ensure their master's victory, but their magic had been drained, and they were slow.

Columns of light came down through the ceiling and struck places on the floor ahead of where the acolytes moved, and the gods of the council appeared in the flesh.

The disciples gasped. Fenris, catching sight of them out of the corner of his bulging yellow eyes, howled in rage and bit down on Bailey's neck as she kicked his legs and groin and clawed his chest.

The deities easily overpowered the weakened demigods, binding them with powerful magic and thrusting them aside.

The two giant beasts, both gods of wolves, separated and circled each other, their teeth and claws bloody.

Like I said, Bailey asserted, speaking with her mind rather than her voice, *I had a surprise waiting. Loki and I set you up, returning the favor. You and Carl killed their illusions, not the real things. They all live, even Thor. He and I sent the World Serpent back to hell. Destiny itself has been changed, and the end of the world is canceled.*

Fenris responded with a psychic message of his own, but not in words. It was no more than a discordant noise representing the unadulterated desire to kill. He pounced.

Bailey dodged to the side. Rather than strike him with fang or paw, she hit him with an invisible tendril that locked into his chest.

If she could drain his power, there would be no way he could perform the ritual. He could sacrifice neither her nor himself.

Fenris recognized her game instantly and resisted, blocking the conduit. He was the one who'd taught her how to do it, after all, and he retained enough of his intelligence to think fast. He bowled into her, slamming her into the ground repeatedly with his forelegs while she bit his limbs and kicked viciously at his underbelly.

Balder called, "Bailey! Remember, I gave you a tool for this moment. It's time!"

The sword.

The girl shifted back into human form, heedless of her sudden nakedness. Smaller, she rolled between Fenris' legs and vaulted into the air, extending her hand. The sacred blade flew from its place in the wall, where she'd left it between a demigod's shoulders, and found its way to her grip.

Fenris lunged. Recalling every piece of information she'd ever acquired about the art of combat and processing it all at once, the girl made a gamble, intending to end the fight.

She calculated her speed and how much time she had. She calculated Fenris' velocity and trajectory and the space closing between them. Between him and the sword. She remembered all the dumbass bar fights she'd been in, and the tricks Balder and Coyote and Fenris had taught her, and her mock fights at the academy.

Somehow, she positioned herself so the colossal fangs and claws missed her, as well as the bulk of the great furry body and the crackling streams of dark magic emanating from his eyes and mouth. Her body stood perfectly in the place where none of them hit.

But she did not miss. The sword's blade pierced the bottom of the monster's jaw, pinning his mouth shut.

Fenris made a horrible low gurgly squawking sound, and his eyes bulged.

Bailey maintained her grip as she had against Jörmungandr the World Serpent, but this time she channeled the stolen power into herself, or into the substratum of Asgard, bleeding Fenris' evil essence and weakening him until he was less than a god.

The sword can't kill him outright this way, she recalled, *but it can bring him down to the point where I can.*

Her body appeared clothed in light as the other god's power drained and flashed through the room. Fenris shifted back into human form, mutating in halted steps rather than changing instantly, with the blade still lodged under his chin.

She knew it was over; Fenris' power had been broken forever. He was reduced to the level of a mere mortal wizard, ineligible for sacrifice. She retracted the sword and he fell to his knees, once again a hooded man, though he looked smaller and thinner. He clutched his hands to his bleeding throat.

The gods watched. Bailey stood before him, the light about her body having coalesced into shimmering white robes.

"Bailey," said Loki, "you mustn't kill him here. The ritual is still in effect. It would consider him an inadequate sacrifice, and we'd have a *partial* Ragnarök. Bring him outside."

She seized the former wolf-father by the shoulder and dragged him out of the throne room. The deities and the imprisoned demigods followed. With no magical beings nearby to draw upon, the sigils in the chamber went dead, and the dark powers that Fenris had called up dissipated into eternity.

Everyone stopped in the main entrance hall of the palace. The friends Bailey had left behind were still there, alive and unharmed. Tyr had shown up, too.

The god of justice proclaimed, "By all the laws and codes of honor of our world, which shall *not* come to an end, Fenris must die for his crimes. Bailey, we feel you should carry out his execution."

The girl's powers had advanced to such a lofty point that she felt distant from the goings-on. Her head was in the proverbial clouds, but she brought herself back and focused on the defeated figure before her.

Fenris had fallen to his knees. He raised his hands and

drew back his hood, exposing his grim, craggy face. He breathed in and coughed blood, then spoke.

"I accept your judgment," he stated.

The girl stared into his eyes. "Why, Fenris? Why did you do this? I would have rather had you as a friend than an enemy. You were like a third father to me. Did you ever truly understand us? Mortals, I mean, and Weres, who are more like humans than gods. We followed you and loved you. Did you love us back?"

The former deity of her people narrowed his eyes. He seemed somber and confused.

"I was not made to love. Observing you, I think I understood it in part. You were my greatest project. You succeeded beyond anything I could have hoped. *Too well.* But destiny decreed that I was not to sit on the council despite my wisdom and power. I was only to be an outcast and either win my own world or perish in the attempt. Now fate has played out. My end is nigh. I would rather have no one finish it than you."

Bailey looked down and closed her eyes. A lump formed in her throat, but she swallowed it at once. Pangs of regret went through her, nearly robbing her of her dignity before all the people watching.

Her mentor's mistake had been to care only about the world to come—the new one he felt *should* exist. Anger had blinded him. He hadn't accepted the world as it was or appreciated the good that was already in it.

She had.

"Goodbye, Fenris," she said.

Bailey swung the sword. The tall man's head rolled from his shoulders into a corner, and the broad-shouldered body stayed perched on its knees for a moment before toppling over. Then both erupted in a cascade of dark-indigo-purple light flecked with moonlight-silver before fading into pools of shadow that sank and were gone.

CHAPTER EIGHTEEN

Odin's throne room had cleaned up nicely, she decided.

The magical sigils had been removed from the floor, the bloodstains scrubbed out, and the damage to the walls repaired. For obscure reasons, it was brighter and airier as well, despite the absence of windows.

Odin still slept and could not attend, but the other gods summoned the full regalia so as to perform their induction ceremony in style.

The Honor Guard of the Palace of Asgard was present in regal dress, lining the walls as well as the long red carpet that formed a path to the dais in the empty throne room. Trumpeters blew majestic notes on their golden horns as the gods of the Nordic pantheon filed in.

Coyote and Thoth were there too, though they originated from other pantheons. Their long friendship and collaboration with the Asgardians and important places on the council more than entitled them to attend.

Behind them came Bailey "Nova" Nordin, resplendent

in a dress of shining mail and a slim circlet-crown. She couldn't remember the last time she'd been dressed so elegantly. The trumpets blew another fanfare as she walked down the carpet toward the platform.

She took her position next to Freya, whom Loki had hidden when Fenris had moved against her. The goddess of sorcery seemed calmer, perhaps due to knowing she'd have her council seat back soon.

Balder and Loki took the floor, raising their hands for attention as the hall grew silent.

"We have splendid news," said the god of beauty, "Bailey is hereby confirmed as a full member of the Nordic pantheon. The werewitch goddess, the Lady of Wolves and Witches. The portfolios of stewardship over both peoples have been unified within her. Thus shall she reign in the place formerly occupied by Fenris Wolf-Father."

The trumpeters blew another triumphant note.

Loki spoke next. "She is a goddess in multiple forms and shall reign across multiple modes of existence. We recognize them all, relieving her of her seat on the council but accepting her input, allowing her instead to reign on Earth, her original home, and the place where she is able to do the most good."

Cheers and applause went around as the two gods lifted Bailey's hands in the air. The other deities came up to congratulate her. Coyote with his subtle, good-natured smile of secret humor. Thoth with his air of old and dignified wisdom. The recovered Thor, his old boisterous self again, with Mjölnir back on his shoulder. Tyr, handless but proud and stern. And Freya, severe-faced but calm and gracious.

Bailey took the floor next. "Thank you all," she began, "for your help, and for your faith in me. I never would have thought I'd have made it this far or achieved so much. I didn't achieve it alone, that's for sure. As a member of the pantheon, I promise to work with the other gods to deal with major problems, and I'll see to it that werewolves and witches aren't at each other's throats but that both work together for the good of the world."

She felt like it wasn't much of a speech, but everyone cheered anyway. It said what she felt needed to be said.

Loki sidled up to her. "Where will you go next? We have no immediate need of you. I suppose it's pointless to ask, in truth."

She grinned. "It is. I'm going home."

A quarter of the town had crowded onto the Nordin family's property.

People were distributed equally between the front yard, the backyard, and the house, though most of them kept drifting out back, where the grills were set up. People drank beer, laughed, ate, and talked. It was the official first day of autumn, warm but with a cool edge to the breeze.

Bailey mingled freely. She was in jeans and boots and a t-shirt, and it was strange to think she'd been outfitted in the universe's finest formal wear not long ago. She was looking forward to peace and quiet in the near future, but for today, she was happy to schmaltz it up with so many familiar and beloved faces.

"See," Kurt began, as Sheriff Browne looked at him with

a skeptical half-frown, "you could start deputizing Weres and have your own werewolf militia as an auxiliary to the police department. Like, we handle the supernatural stuff, and you deal with normal shit. Imagine the possibilities!"

The sheriff made a grumbling sound. "I'll think about it. Last thing we need is a bunch of vigilantes, but this town has a way of attracting trouble."

Bailey waved a hand. "I'll head off as much trouble as I can, so it becomes a moot point."

Kurt pretended neither of them had spoken. "And, see, since we'd operate outside of the normal law, we could lower the drinking age for members!"

Jacob threw a crushed beer cup at him, which ricocheted off his younger brother's head. "Shut up, Kurt. You can wait 'til you're twenty-one like everyone else instead of concocting an elaborate boondoggle to trick the sheriff into letting you get plastered."

Agents Park and Velasquez snickered at that, while Townsend smirked as he sat behind them at an old picnic table.

Velasquez said, "Your brother's creative. That's potentially a good thing."

"But," Park added, "they *should* lower the drinking age. I was in the Army at nineteen, but for some frickin' reason, it took another two years before I could buy a beer."

Browne shrugged. "Talk to Salem. Or Washington. All I do is enforce laws, not make them."

Gunney had loitered at the edge of the crowd. He'd never been entirely comfortable at parties; he was more at home in his shop or behind the wheel. Still, there was no way he was going to miss the current one. Bailey went over and gave him a hug.

"Thanks for showing up, you greasy old coot." She pushed a beer into his hands.

"Yeah, yeah," he retorted. "Thanks for making me come, you trouble-making female canine-type entity. I think there's a word for that."

She laughed. "Shut up. Save that kind of talk for the pit. This is a family gathering."

He snorted. "I suppose it is. But thank *you* for keeping all the things that go bump in the night from destroying my damn shop and my yard out back time and again. End of the world would have taken a lot of fine cars with it."

Bailey bumped into Will Waldsbach, who was completely shit-faced, and patted him on the back before directing him to the water cooler. She was glad he was okay. He stumbled into a conversation with Tomi, the full-time evening waitress at the Elk, who was equally drunk and feeling flirtatious.

Then she headed toward three men who'd been conferring in low voices. One of them, Alfred the shaman, was doing most of the talking, seemingly in response to questions from the other two.

"I can perform the wedding ceremony as soon as—" His eyes snapped up and he closed his mouth as he saw Bailey approach, though he retained a faint look of amusement.

The two with him were Bailey's husband-to-be and her father.

Nordin the elder put his hand on his daughter's shoulder. "Bailey. You know I'm proud of you, though I'm not around to say it as much as I should be. It's always been easy to get distracted by other things around here."

He was a tall, rangy man, not dissimilar in appearance from his children, though the hard years had taken their toll. His long, lined face was warmer and happier than usual.

She gave him a brief but sincere hug. "It's okay, Dad. The valley would be lost without you fixing their shit and presiding over obscure pack politics. Good thing your sons aren't complete morons and know how to manage the house."

He laughed gently. "Not so sure about that."

Roland took the girl by the arm. "Lovely party," he remarked, "but I think it will survive without us. Let's decamp to that scenic outlook. The one that requires us to take *two* cars." His eyes flashed.

Bailey glared at him but smiled. "Oh, I see. A race again, is it?"

"Exactly." He hid his cup behind his back. "I only had one and a quarter drinks, so I'll be fine."

She glanced to see if the sheriff had heard, but he was still distracted by Kurt's ramblings. "Okay, you're on."

Soon, the Camaro and the Audi sat side by side at the base of the road that led up into the eastern foothills and around the peak where the scenic overlook awaited. No other motorists were nearby, and the day's light was waning.

Roland leaned out his window and waved his hand. "Ready, set, *go*."

Both of them pounded their feet on gas pedals, the cars

pulling out with a satisfying squeal of rubber and back-blasts of blue smoke.

They were neck and neck at first. As the asphalt narrowed and they entered the no-passing zone where the road bent around the base of the mountain, the werewitch saw an opening to pull ahead of her lover's white Audi.

But she didn't.

Gunney had told her that occasionally it was better to let the other person win. It was impossible to say why, but that seemed like a good idea right now. Perhaps because Roland was the one who suggested the race, and she wanted him to be happy.

He pulled past her, smiling and cackling in triumph, and she pretended to scowl at his rear bumper.

A few minutes later, Roland pulled into the overlook's broad parking area half a second ahead of her. His tires screeched again as he brought the vehicle to a hasty stop.

"Hah!" He leapt out of his car. "I knew I'd get you sooner or later. I'm moving up in the world."

She stepped out and regarded him with her tongue moving around her teeth and her fists on her hips. "Horse-shit. I let you win, city boy. Was afraid your one-and-a-quarter beers would impair your driving ability if you had to try too hard."

He flapped a hand. "Nonsense. But victory has put me in a gracious mood, so come over here while I perform a magic trick. Not a demigod-level spell, but the kind that involves pulling things out of your sleeve and so forth."

Blinking in confusion, the girl watched as Roland turned away, fished around in his clothes, and spun back toward her. In his hand was a small square black box, open.

Within it on a tiny white cushion sat a golden ring set with a glimmering diamond.

"Behold," he exclaimed, "my mysterious powers of sorcery!"

Bailey gawked at it stupidly. "How the hell did you afford that? You don't even have a job, boy. When we first met, you were a goddamn credit card fraudster. You didn't steal it, did you? Sorry, not trying to ruin the moment. It's beautiful."

He made a pouty face. "Of course not. I paid for part of it myself, but otherwise, it's the fruits of a crowdfunding campaign amongst the Seattle and Portland witch communities. Dante and Charlene came up with the idea. No, really. It's a gift from all of them to us. *Shannon* contributed five whole dollars to something that indicates that I'm marrying someone *else!* If there's hope for her, there's hope for anyone."

She accepted it, admiring the sparkly stone and the fine craftsmanship of the ring. "I love it," she said. "And you, of course."

Their hands locked together, and their lips followed suit. She felt giddy; it had been too long since she'd been this happy. The future opened up before her, and she found that she was looking forward to it.

"So," she asked, "when do you want to get married?"

Roland reflected, his eyes going out of focus for five or six seconds. "Soon," he declared. "We'll have to go through all the rigmarole first, but let's start that next week after we relax a bit. I'd say we've earned another vacation."

Bailey kissed him again, longer and deeper than previously, and they touched foreheads as their mouths separated. "Deal," she replied.

Then they turned, arm in arm, and watched the sun go down over the mountains and forests that sprawled over their corner of the world.

The End

Have you read the **Callie Heart** series from Renée Jaggér? Book one in the series is *Thin Ice,* and it's available from Amazon and other digital book stores

Grab your copy today!

You made it! Here we are at the end of book 9, last in the series. Thank you so much for reading this far.

This series has been a labor of love since I have always liked the Norse pantheon. Fleshing them out has been fun, as well as attributing all too human behaviors to them. Basically, I always felt they could just be the Vikings next door when I read the tales, and in this series, they more or less are. They scheme, intrigue, and bicker like everyone we have ever met, as well as believing their plans will succeed when we know they won't.

Maybe I should go to Scandinavia for my trip next year. Nah, the idea is to be someplace warm, and this series is over. On to the next!

Since this is my last opportunity for a while, I wish you and yours the best of luck with this whole Covid-19 thing. I hope you are unscathed so far and remain so. To a Vaccine and Beyond! Unless you're anti-vax, then No Vaccine and Beyond!

Meanwhile, back at the house, the hot tub is in and is

being much enjoyed, and I am finalizing my plans to go to the area around Split, Croatia for two or three months next year, starting in May. I have a house in a small village with a deck over the Adriatic, and Jo and Storm will be spoiled at their grandmother's. Several of my friends will be joining me on my overseas adventure, so look forward to tales of our doings in future *Author Notes*! Not sure what series is coming next, but there will be one, and there will be *Author Notes*! And Beyond!

My profound thanks, as always, go to my advance readers and the proofreader team, the ones who read my stories after they are edited. They help make this book (and every book) its best. Couldn't do it without you, folks! Much appreciated!

I hope you enjoyed Bailey's and Roland's further adventures. I am taking a break from writing for a while while I pursue some other projects. I hope to be back within six months. If you get a moment, drop me a review, please. Those keep us writers going! We are very grateful when a fan takes the time to do that for us, and for other people who may want to venture into our world!

Until next time,
Renée

I COULDN'T DO THIS WITHOUT YOU!

Thanks to my early readers, you rock!

Jeff Goode, Dorothy Lloyd, Angel LaVey, Diane L. Smith,
Dave Hicks, James Caplan

CONNECT WITH THE AUTHOR

Renée Jaggér Social

Website:
https://reneejagger.com/

Facebook Here:
https://www.facebook.com/reneejaggerauthor/

The WereWitch Series
Bad Attitude (Book One)
A Bit Aggressive (Book Two)
Too Much Magic (Book Three)
Were War (Book Four)
Were Rages (Book Five)
God Ender (Book Six)
God Trials (Book Seven)
The Troll Solution (Book Eight)
Winner Takes All (Book Nine)

Callie Hart Series
Thin Ice (Book One)
Cold Blood (Book Two)
Feelings Run Deep (Book Three)